The Studhorse Man

Other books by Robert Kroetsch

Alberta
The Words of my Roaring
But we are Exiles

Robert
Kroetsch

The
Studhorse
Man

Macmillan of Canada, Toronto

First published in Great Britain 1969
by Macdonald & Co. (Publishers) Ltd,
49–50 Poland Street, London W.1

First published in Canada by
The Macmillan Company of Canada
70 Bond Street Toronto 2

SBN 356 02855 0

Made and printed in Great Britain by
Unwin Brothers Limited
Woking and London

Set in Monotype Plantin

To Dick Martin and Norman Freeman

'Allas! allas! that evere love was synne!'
—Chaucer's Good Wife of Bath

I

Hazard had to get hold of a mare. He was desperate. In an area centred on a string of seven towns he was the only remaining studhorse man, yet in the previous season he had travelled the hundreds of miles of dirt roads in a two-wheeled cart, pulled by his old gelding, leading his beautiful blue beast of a virgin stallion

—and he had found not one farmer with a mare that wanted covering.

He was a truly desperate man. Extinction or survival was quite simply to be the fate of the breed of horse he alone had preserved through six generations; thus, penniless as he was, and he had been reduced to living on porridge for nearly a month, he hit on the scheme of somehow buying a mare. With commendable determination he found a neighbour who would sell his single remaining horse for $20.00—upon closing his fist on spot cash. 'No money, no mare,' the unkind neighbour commented to clinch the deal, as if Hazard might not be financially reliable.

Fortunately, the war was in progress; the government was scouring Alberta for bones. BONES FOR WAR, the ads and posters read:

BRING IN YOUR BONES
WE PAY CASH

In the same newspaper that carried this federal proclamation is a notice from an uncle of mine saying he planned to be in the town of Burkhardt from Thursday, 8 March, to Saturday, 10 March, with the patriotic intent of purchasing all available loads of scrap iron, rags, bones, and miscellaneous. Hazard, travelling the countryside as was his wont, knew where to find every skeleton of a cow, every buffalo skull, even, it must be added, every carcass of a horse. He read my uncle's notice and in twenty-five days gathered together a pile of bones that he guessed to be worth at least as many dollars.

Thus it was that on Thursday, 8 March, Hazard Lepage got out of bed three hours earlier than usual—he was sleeping in his fifth bed, the significance of which I shall explore later—he made his porridge and tea, combed his hair and beard, put on his overshoes and mackinaw and fur cap, and precisely at 8.15 he went outside to dig a hole in the snowbank covering his recently accumulated pile of bones.

8

By 10.10 he was kicking around in the powdered snow, hitting almost nothing. He found a horse's skull, knocked it clean on the sleigh's bolster, tossed it on to the pile that now humped out of the sleigh's weathered green box. He gave one last kick, found a jawbone, and then, knocking the snow off his wet leather mitts, out of his beard, he crawled up from the hole he had by this time dug to a depth of nearly six feet. He cursed rather freely the pain in his back.

Shading his eyes against the really blinding glare (they were brown eyes, dark, large; eyes that compelled women to speak, it would appear), he looked out across the Cree River valley and Wildfire Lake towards the horizon. An arch of pale blue sky held off the white fur of cloud from the tree-scratched white of the low hills. Obviously, the chinook was set to blow for hours.

Hazard recognized that the snow cover must quickly vanish from the roads. He hurried to his giant, square box of a house: a mansion-like affair, it was surrounded on three sides by verandas, one above the other, giving the effect of the house deck of a sternwheeler. He limped up the gangplank he now used in place of the veranda steps; he waited when his wet palm stuck to the huge iron knocker; then he was inside and warm in the sunlit hallway.

The thought of departing was somehow and suddenly unbearable. Perhaps he remembered the days when he could take his leave relaxed in the knowledge that in one week a dozen mares might be stinted to his horse. God knows, we have all confronted failure. But Hazard, instead of hurrying to harness his team, took off his mackinaw; he went into the dining room and opened the bay window—and quietly, without haste, he cleaned the pile of steaming turds from behind the gelding, pitched them out of the window, put down fresh straw. Then he went into the parlour; at his leisure he built behind Poseidon a pyramid of turds on a pad of straw; and lifting his creation on a four-tined fork—I have used the fork myself, its handle worn bright and smooth by love—he returned fastidiously to the adjacent room and the open window.

The town of Burkhardt, directly north from the mansion, is

distant a hard day's drive through small poplar groves and across open prairie; the snow was certain to go fast. Hazard could not long deny this to himself; after currying both the gelding and the stallion he went into the library, lifted down a set of harness from the left horn of a buffalo's head, and quickly he harnessed the gelding, Prince. But his back, distressed by his recent efforts, was sending flashes of pain down both legs.

On returning to the library for the second set of harness he sat down momentarily on a long leather chesterfield facing the roll-top desk. Hazard dearly loved to read. His poetry and his philosophy were a leatherbound, stained, ancient collection called *The General Stud Book*. The Englishman who built the isolated mansion and perished within its walls had brought the volumes with him from God-knows what elegant manor house or dusty London bookshop. Those volumes were Hazard's history of man and his theology. Sitting, he could not help but confront the chaos on the bookshelves beside the desk: currycombs, a broken hame-strap, a spoon wired to a stick for dropping poisoned wheat into the holes of offending gophers, saltpetre, gentian root, a scattering of copper rivets, black antimony, a schoolboy's ruler, three mousetraps in a matchbox, two chisels for trimming hoofs, Cornucrescine (for making horn grow), ginger, horse liniment and liniment for his back, Elliman's Royal Embrocation, blue vitriol, an electuary, nux vomica, saddle soap in a Spode (a simple blue and white) saucer, Spanish fly—

He pulled down the first volume from the one neat row of books. The old book opened of itself to the list of brood mares, and Hazard read defiantly the words he could so easily quote: ALCIDES MARE, *Bred by Mr Bland, in 1764, her dam by Crab, out of Snap's dam.* Hazard, let me explain, was no loafing, snivelling school-marm of a man: those words were pain to him. Those beautiful words. He read on: BLANK MARE, *Foaled in 1755, her dam, Dizzy, by Driver* . . . Don't you see why he read, why he ached, why he had to read? Let me go on, for I, too, on sleepless nights, on lonely afternoons, have sought out that dark volume: *Dizzy, by Driver—Smiling Tom—Miss Hipp, by Oysterfoot—*

Merlin—Commoner—D. of Somerset's Coppin Mare. Not that Hazard wept as I have. Hazard cursed. 'God damn the damned,' he said. Forgive me if I am sometimes enthralled by his very crudeness. Yet as you can well imagine, even as he repeated quietly to me what he had said in passion, even as he chuckled over the beer I had discreetly provided, he injured me deeply. He denied the past; 'God damn the damned,' he repeated; and there I sat, pencil in hand, notebook on my lap, already devoting my life to the making of his present into history.

But I am happy now, conjuring up a huge head and a bearded face bent over that book. He must have put a stained finger to the old print. He cursed and read on, caught in and dreading that beautiful dead mad century: A-LA-GRECQUE . . . *got by Regulus —her dam by Allworthy—grandam by the Bolton Starling—great grandam, Dairy Maid, by Bloody Buttocks—great great grandam, Bay Brocklesby, by Old Partner—great great great grandam, Brocklesby, by Greyhound* . . .

And he needed one mare, as I say; or the Lepage horse was extinct.

He harnessed Poseidon. There in that strange, lost parlour, the walls patterned white and blue and gold with alternating lions and fleurs-de-lis, the high ceiling stained with the smoke from great gushing streams of hot piss. He put a collar to his stallion's neck, a Liverpool bit to the fine strong mouth. Hazard was a lonely man, surely. He was not above talking to horses. Indeed, what a biography that horse could have inscribed on the insufferable blank pages of time—the horse that listened then. 'Yuh, Posse, take it from me,' Hazard said; he variously shortened the true name to Posse or Poesy or Pussy. 'I'll tell you the whole sad truth of it. We've got to go, but I mean it: the studhorse business isn't so good.' He turned to relieve himself before venturing again into the weather, using for his convenience an arched and marble fireplace, his very prodigality echoing into the chimney's tall darkness. Politely he shielded—Old Blue, as he was fond of remarking, when in a jovial mood. 'Whoever thought,' he went on, fumbling a button into its hole, 'that screwing would go out of style? But it did, it is . . .'

2

Hazard, in his pessimistic moments, had a most preposterous fear of death. Why any man should fear so comic an adversary I find hard to fathom. But at least he felt secure in his old house; it was the road he dreaded—travel. And as you shall discover, this dread was not without some little foundation. But he harnessed the stallion, nevertheless, he hooked his team to the sleigh, and climbing up on his load of bones he struck out for town.

Perhaps I need elaborate before we pursue him: Hazard feared especially death at sea. A woman had prophesied that fate for him: an old woman on the battlefields of France during the Great War. He was twenty-three at the time; it was during the battle for Passchendaele Ridge. Hazard found her sitting blue-eyed between two naked corpses in a flooded cellar. '*Mon pauvre soldat, inutile de te cacher,*' she whispered—or at least her old voice came like the hoot of a far-off owl against the thump of gunfire. '*La mer sera votre meurtrière.*' The sea shall be your murderess. Hazard was first aware only of the two square miles of mud for which the infantry were trading sixteen thousand casualties. When he told me of the incident he recalled further the water lapping at the old woman's button shoes, the sea-glitter of an emerald ring, the soldier's helmet she wore on her apparently old and yet so beautiful head. It was twenty minutes after this encounter that he first hurt his back, while removing his bayonet from a German captain.

There was just enough snow on the streets of Burkhardt so he might get through town to the railway and the gate of the stockyards. It was twilight now; he pulled up to the gate. A banner overhead snapped in a small wind, a canvas banner; BONES FOR WAR it bellied in the wind, snapping across a red sky. Hazard drove in under the sign.

Thirty and more trucks and sleighs and wagons waited in ragged line to unload. 'Whoa, boys,' Hazard said to his team. 'Easy, Poseidon. Easy, Poesy, boy. Easy, Prince.'

The gelding, glad for the rest, held the stallion. The reins and bit couldn't hold him; the scent of spring was in that yeasty wind, the high raw odour of mares and spring –

Already I find myself straying from the mere facts. I distort. I must control a certain penchant for gentleness and beauty. Hazard did not say 'mares and spring'. We were chatting together on the ranch where finally I caught up with him and he said in his crude way, 'that raw bitch of a wind was full of crocuses and snatch'.

But a cane was tapping at the sleigh box. 'Okay, okay.' The cane itself might have been speaking. 'Let's consider—'

'Good evening,' Hazard said. He leaned forward, stiff from sitting too long, catching at a thighbone to keep from losing his balance on his high load.

'Bad news and a hell of a day.'

'A pippin of a lovely day,' Hazard replied.

'Grim ghastly news for you if you listened to the radio, Mac.' The cane rose in the hanging darkness and touched Hazard's arm; the sturdy kind of cane that cattle buyers use. 'Old Hazard! Whiskers and all! You dirty rascal!'

That's when Hazard recognized, as well he should have, the eldest of the Proudfoot boys: a hugely fat man in a black overcoat. Tad is my uncle, Martha Proudfoot's uncle: it was he who most violently opposed the engagement of Martha to Hazard.

'Hell—hello. Hazard Lepage! The rottenest bad buggering news for you. The goddamn Yanks have crossed the Rhine.' Uncle Tad struck hard at the sleigh box with his cane. 'The market for bone meal and fertilizer is shot right now or I'm a two-faced liar. You, Hazard, have just wasted—' Uncle Tad grinned wickedly, a wad of Copenhagen making a lump under his wet lower lip. 'Your horses will really be worthless now.'

Hazard, with the thighbone in his right hand, indicated Poseidon. 'The next generation of this breed, I am willing to lay heavy odds, will be worth more than a Morgan stallion. All I need is one mare that is worthy of the honour—'

'You need a car,' Tad corrected.

'Okay, okay—' Hazard checked himself. 'But a little hard cash will do for now.' He nodded around at his load of bones.

Tad was shaking his bright bald head, shaking with it the purple sky. 'No. Yup. Okay. I'll give you two bucks for the load. If you agree to unload them.'

'It's a deal,' Hazard said. He pretended to reach towards the peg on which he had tied the reins. 'If you ram them up your ass without any help from me.'

'Throw in the team,' Tad said, 'and I'll make it ten.' He rapped his own head. 'But you'll have to provide the shotgun and shells.'

'I'll need a strong team,' Hazard said, 'to haul you up on top of that.' He indicated a mound of unloaded bones that faded off into the closing horizon.

'For Christsake listen,' Tad said. 'I'm offering you ten bucks just to take them off your hands. Once gas rationing is over and tractors are back on the market, you won't be able to *give* a horse away. So I'll do you a big favour—twenty bucks even for the bones, team and sleigh.'

That's when Hazard swung the bone that was in his right hand. It was certainly nothing malicious; Hazard wasn't half my uncle's weight. But Tad was quicker than anyone guessed: the next thing Hazard knew he was wearing the end of a cane around his neck, the muddy frozen ground was coming up so fast he didn't have time to shield his face.

Then a dozen drivers and teamsters were standing around the two men. A hoof sailed in from the surrounding shadows and hit Tad's chest. But Tad didn't flinch. He used his cane to hoist Hazard to his feet, hooking it into an armpit, raising his left hand at the same time to signal for silence.

'How do we know the market is kaput?' a teamster said, picking up Hazard's fur cap and setting it cockeyed on the poor man's head. Hazard at this point was not without supporters; only later, was he to have only me. 'Cuts your profits in half, Proudfoot', someone dared to say from outside the immediate group.

To keep the record straight: Tad paid the farmer from five to $15.00 a ton, and sold to a Chicago firm for $50.00. The catch was, I suppose, that it was Tad himself who estimated the weight of a load. 'Okay, okay,' he was saying. 'This nut here—' he pointed his cane at the team, then at Hazard—'keeps horses in his *house*.'

'It's a free country,' a big Métis truck driver said.

Even Tad had to smile.

'Don't give us that song and dance,' a voice insisted, somehow distant in the peculiar darkness that lay like a mist beneath the streaked and blue-black sky. 'You bone-mongering profiteer, Proudfoot.'

'In his house,' Tad repeated. 'In his *house*. Maybe you gentlemen live that way. But I can honestly say that *I* and my sons don't. His goddamn house is full of creosote and horse turds.'

The men in the circle burst out laughing, their sudden joy a clamour of crows.

'This crazy bastard is going to marry my niece,' Tad said. 'Just as soon as he gets his house ready for the bride. Just as soon as he gets rich.'

The teamster who a moment earlier had been muttering against Uncle Tad now poked at a hole in the back of Hazard's green mackinaw, hooked in a finger and ripped.

'Look at the weasling bastard,' Tad said. 'Why don't you shave, Lepage?' He straightened Hazard's cap with his cane. 'I'll tell you why, Lepage, my boy. You're too damned lazy! You won't *work*. You won't earn an honest dollar. With these men right here short of help. Why the hell aren't you in the army?'

Hazard, instead of explaining that he'd hurt his back recovering a bayonet from an enemy soldier whose rank was much higher than his own, responded simply, 'Thou shalt not kill.'

'You're a damned coward frog,' Tad said.

So Hazard again was left with little choice. He turned as if to walk away; he picked up a horse's rib that lay in a puddle on a patch of ice; he turned back and in the confusion of men and darkness quietly struck my uncle, Tad Proudfoot, a blow between his small red glowing eyes, set too close together in his broad face, and floored him.

The sky began to rain bones. It was impossible to know who was on whose side. Some men were irritated with my uncle for not paying them a living wage for their bones; some were merely concerned to vent their (I use the jargon of my favourite shrink) frustration. The chief end was to strike and to strike hard. Hazard himself kicked at the fallen Tad Proudfoot, aiming carefully for his balls. But it was like kicking a sack of oats. At best you could hope to sprain an ankle.

It was the bones that did the most damage. Flying through the air as if they must have wings, swooping and whistling, they scared Hazard's team. He had to dive for the sleigh and crawl up through a bludgeoning crossfire to free the reins. And now Poseidon's whinnying had set other teams to breaking loose.

Men cursed and grunted against the flood of darkness. Wheel hubs rammed at sleigh boxes. Harness jangled as it tore and broke. Hazard was hit just below his right eye by a large object that knocked him off the sleigh's doubletree. While picking himself up he picked up also the object that had injured him, assuming he might find it of some use.

'Okay, okay,' Tad was shouting now, directing his forces, especially the men he had hired to load his mounds of bones into boxcars. 'We've got to show this yellow-belly.' He waved his cane upright before his own stomach as he led his doughty band. 'This peasoup loafer. This hairy lunatic.' Tad was making the kind of irresponsible remark that absolutely infuriates me. 'This maniac who peddles horse cock from farm to farm when nobody wants horses.'

Hazard crawled or was knocked in behind his team, and while there he unhooked them, risking his life between the sleigh runners and Poseidon's heels. He had both horses unhooked, the traces hanging loose, and then he must go around to let down the neck yoke.

That's when Tad saw the object held like a bowling ball in Hazard's left hand. 'Look at this, men. Look here, men, look. This bearded madman is attacking us with a skull.'

Hazard's gesture of denial raised into place a human skull, the lipless grin full of teeth, the ears strangely absent. The Métis, as if he had been waiting, struck a match, and just as the light flared into the dark sockets, just as maybe a dozen, twenty men bent close, Tad whispered in the new silence: 'You ought to be put away, Lepage. You dug—' He coughed, breathing hard, and spat clean through a socket. 'You robbed that grave in your cellar.'

The whole mob turned on Hazard: the match was knocked out and maybe thirty men were falling over each other in the plastic grip of darkness, hitting each other as they tried to get at Hazard. He bellowed and turned, trying to fight his way clear. He swung the skull, clubbing men down in his fury to protect himself; he struggled and dodged as men stomped over each other trying to get at him, snatching at his torn mackinaw, punching and pushing—and he caught at Poseidon's bridle, the bones and fists slashing him now; half delirious he was shouting to Poseidon; and then Poseidon went up on his hind legs, magnificent and beautiful, terrible to the men cowering beneath him; he reared up taking Hazard with him, Hazard hanging on for dear life with one hand, dangling up there above those turncoat bastards, the lines tearing away from Prince, the loyal gelding nervous but trying to hold Poseidon steady, trying to stop him; then Poseidon lunged at a mare that was ten yards away, caught in harness and a wheel, and Hazard was carried along, still trying to control, trying to guide.

He couldn't turn Poseidon; he couldn't get him near that flapping canvas: BONES FOR WAR it snapped overhead. He couldn't turn that great charging blue beast of a stallion; the mares, two or three of them, fighting their harness in their own awakened eagerness, whinnied and hunched away from his teeth.

And then Hazard saw a patch of darkness that was darker than all the black around him. He pulled at Poseidon's bridle, hung on, running as he was dragged along, the horse striking out with his head and hoofs, men screaming and running, rolling in the mud and shattered ice to get out of the way, cursing and yelling for mercy, still throwing bones, some of them—and somehow they were up the ramp, Poseidon and Hazard: they dodged into the boxcar, stumbled over the heaped bones. He was heaving his whole weight at the door, trying to roll it shut. Then, even as he gave up all hope, it began to move; and he stepped ahead of the moving door to fire the skull. And just as he might have let go something sharp struck him full on the forehead, the door rolling shut, the stallion whinnying, pawing, threatening to scatter him into death, the lock on the door clacking, echoing then, farther and farther away, miles away. And he was embracing the bones, gently, blindly embracing the hard bones, dreaming the flesh, embracing already a dreamed woman, the soft large breasts of Martha, those breasts no man could drive from his dreaming—he was afloat and drifting on a great tangle and raft of pale and hardened and dream-soft bones –

3

This Martha, of whom you shall be learning quite a good deal, is my first cousin, Martha Proudfoot of Coulee Hill. Hazard had kept the poor girl waiting for thirteen years while he, penniless, yet not without some peculiar fascination for others, not only neglected my dear cousin but took advantage of this fascination to exploit the frailty of no end of women. Martha would surely have been happier had she never met him; but her family kept a hotel and livery barn and the meeting was somehow inevitable.

While a biographer must naturally record, he must also, of necessity, be interpretive upon occasion. I have in my possession, for instance, notes on Hazard's dreams. He spoke freely, even jokingly, of what he dreamt during that ghastly night. Yet those notes are without significance until we probe them for invisible meanings.

He imagined that an Indian in a breech-cloth and a messenger's red cap rode a bicycle through the boxcar door.

'You may remember me,' the Indian said. 'I'm buried in that patch of spruce directly below the cliff from your mansion.'

'Of course,' Hazard said. 'I have protected your grave against all marauders, animal and human.'

'I appreciate your concern,' the Indian said.

'Not at all,' Hazard said, 'the pleasure is mine. That little circle of stones is a solace to me. Of an evening I sometimes visit you. I have on occasion spoken briefly.'

'I appreciate your concern,' the Indian repeated. 'But if it's no trouble I would like my skull.'

'No trouble at all', Hazard said. He gave a finely polished skull one last rub for good measure and handed it to the Indian.

'Thank you again, sir.' The Indian began to fade. 'O, by the way,' he said, 'I was asked to give you this.'

'I appreciate it', Hazard said. He took the folded sheet of yellow paper, unfolded it with great care, and read silently to himself: BRING SKULL WITH YOU STOP WHERE ARE ELBOWS KNEES PECKER LOVE MARTHA.

Hazard recognized that he no longer had the skull. 'I must ask you,' he said to the Indian, 'to deliver a message for me.'

'No trouble at all sir,' the Indian said. He drew a pencil and pad from his breech-cloth.

Hazard's dream, no doubt, stemmed from a feeling of guilt; but in his defiance, in his reluctance to acknowledge his misbehaviour in the whole affair with Martha, he dictated to the Indian a reply: CANNOT GET AWAY AM IN COFFIN VERY SORRY REGARDS HAZARD.

'Very well,' the Indian said, tipping his messenger's cap, snapping a clip on to his bare right leg, lifting his leg over his red CCM bicycle. 'That will be twenty dollars, sir.'

He was disappearing, fading through the boxcar door: 'No!' Hazard shouted.

'No!'

He was awakened, not by the many sounds about him, but by his own voice: the darkness in its perfection made him touch two fingers to his eyes—only to discover in turn that his fingers themselves were very nearly beyond sensation. He reached one hand towards where he believed the door to be; then he felt on the wrist of his extended arm the draught by the doorway, the flecks of blown snow: and he realized for the first time that he was travelling.

Now Hazard heard the insistent battering at his ears. He and Poseidon were being flung through the night to the skittish clatter of iron wheels on frosted rails. And Hazard, in a moment of terror, reached out to touch Poseidon—only to insert four fingers directly into the teeth of an invisible jaw.

Here I must confess to a certain lack of sympathy; surely to be confined, to be intimately at one with the immediate environment, is other than terrifying. But Hazard, unthinkingly, shrank from what might have been the pleasure of the situation. He insisted that he was frightened, aching, bitterly chilled, literally numb; yet I note that his response was to squirm deeper into the pile of bones.

He did not so much as attempt one single cry of distress. Rather, he blubbered away to himself, as if being careful that only he should hear. He addressed a few remarks to Martha, for he was under the impression that he was being rushed to the end of the railway line—to Coulee Hill. And to his submission at last.

I should explain that Hazard was not totally to blame for the delay in setting a date for the wedding. Martha herself had sworn she would only marry him when he abandoned the folly of trying to perpetuate his own breed of horse. Again the necessity of interpretation: was Martha only using this as an excuse while she waited for a younger man to recognize the import of his affections? But no, this is neither the time nor the place . . . Martha collected Arab mares, she had security for both her mares and herself in her father's hotel, she asked Hazard to take a position with her father.

'I am breeding the perfect horse,' Hazard said to a heard voice.

'It already exists,' the voice replied.

No wonder he himself was fascinated, he who fascinated others. He tried to argue, to damn the past into the oblivion he felt it richly deserved. 'It exists,' the voice replied, feminine and insistent. He began to argue all the more, lying on his bed of bones.

He pleaded; then he found he was crying, crying mutely in the darkness, every bone of his body a deep throb of pain, the cold stiffening his fists and knees. He was awake and remembering the warmth and laughter of the beer parlour, the heaped dinner table, the warm white beds. 'Posse,' he said to the darkness. 'I hope to heaven, Posse, this train is taking us directly to Coulee Hill.' He rubbed a lump of fist at his freezing tears. 'I am ready to sign. By sundown tomorrow, if we survive this, I'll be a desk clerk and a waiter. I'll be a married man—'

But in the midst of his surrender he experienced a temporary fit of rebellion: he leaned forward in the darkness, rose up with one titanic effort to his knees and threw himself at the locked door. He flung his body against it, the rough and splintered planks scratching his face, flinging back at him the body that was his own. He clawed at the thin crack where the wind sang its not unmusical lament; he chipped his fingernails.

Now he was surely confused. Feeling in the darkness he encountered his own beard: and he remembered the hair of the dead goes on growing. He began to laugh. Ever so softly he chuckled, plunging his stiff hands now between his thighs: Old Blue himself was so shrivelled with the cold as to be apparently gone and vanished. Hazard clapped both hands into his groin. He curled and doubled forward, clinging to, seeking, the one last spark that might revive him. 'Martha,' he cried out. He gasped for air. 'Martha. Martha.' The boxcar rocked him down, down towards submission. Drowning in darkness, in the wind's wail and the infinite clatter of night, he called again, for now he could see her. He saw Martha where she stood, between him and the gate of the skating rink which in summer she used as her corral, the sun behind her setting and red. She was taller than he, standing there motionless; her hips were broad even in the blue smock she wore over her white dress. She did not see him but rather the stallion at his side, the great cock hanging like the pipe from an eaves trough. She shook her head, the nares of her high nose gleaming tensed and white. But she would not look away, would not hear him. Proudly she stood, defying the studhorse man himself: there are virgins and there are virgins. She ignored him, and he could not turn from her big soft body, her great full breasts as soft as a horse's nose.

O how I understand poor Hazard. How I understand. There is no need for interpretation. The bones rattled. There in the darkness the bones chattered and talked. Hazard lay on a winter of bones: skulls and hoofs and hipbones, vertebrae and scapulae, ribs and pelvises and stray jaws with only a few teeth missing, knucklebones in need of only slight repair. The very beast dismantled: bones beat white by the sun, polished by dust on dust, scoured by the slow drift of wind and rain. Bones blasted, dying into the cold earth; bones ploughed from the earth, raised out of the dark by the night's frost. The lost bones of time, cracked and broken, the ache all rotted back into oblivion; only the stark form left, reminding him that pain too is brief and maybe to be treasured. O how I understand. Bones sprouting and growing from the very dark itself.

Hazard put on a green celluloid vizor against the vision that would not speak. She would not hear him; Martha would not speak her recognition but only stared with her sea-green eyes, her cold, imperious, wondering, pleading—O Lord have mercy—condemning green eyes: Hazard put on his vizor and now he tapped a message against her unrelenting gaze; STOP, he hammered on the key. He would not pause now. STOP he sent again. STOP STOP STOP he tapped. He heard the message he must send to Martha. The blizzard blew, the snow drifted into the cattle's coats, the ice closed over their nostrils and eyes. STOP he wired. STOP STOP STOP STOP. Buffalo galloped in a hot roaring frenzy to the cliff's edge beside the lake, by Hazard's mansion; galloped into a moment when it was too late to turn, into a tall and breath-long leap and a hump of twisted necks and broken legs. And the Cree squaws, prouder than men, levelled their silent, killing guns, lunged brave with knives that drew no blood. But the bones rattled, untouched and alone they rattled: STOP STOP he was pleading now. STOP. He took his hand off the key and the key went on sending its single word, on and on it tapped, STOP STOP STOP STOP STOP STOP STOP STOP STOP STOP STOP STOP STOP STOP If she would listen. There were other words he knew he should send: HORSE. Other words: DARKNESS COLD PAIN FEAR ELBOW KNEE HORSE HORSE. If she would just once listen. He could explain: the frost in his beard, the beads of frost, turning the dark white, closing ice over his mouth, his nostrils. He put a hand to the key and the key tapped his hand STOP STOP STOP STOP STOP STOP STOP STOP STOP STOP STOP STOP STOP STOP STOP STOP STOP STOP STOP STOP STOP STOP STOP STOP STOP STOP STOP STOP STOP STOP STOP STOP STOP STOP STOP STOP STOP STOP STOP STOP STOP STOP STOP STOP STOP STOP STOP STOP STOP STOP STOP STOP STOP STOP STOP STOP STOP STOP STOP STOP STOP STOP STOP STOP STOP STOP STOP STOP STOP STOP STOP STOP STOP STOP STOP STOP STOP STOP STOP STOP STOP STOP

4

Hazard became aware first of the smell of burning wool: he raised slightly his head, opened his eyes, and recognized far away his own stockinged feet. Two fine wisps of smoke made snuffed candles of his great toes. The sight pleased him and he was about to lie back in repose: but a cup of coffee splashed into his beard.

'Whoopsee-daisy,' a deep voice said.

'My horse,' Hazard croaked and gurgled against the scalding flow.

'Your horse my ass,' the deep voice said. 'Stop your damned spitting and drink some coffee.'

Hazard sought for his hands and couldn't find them. 'My big blue stallion.'

A striped denim cap came down on his gaze. 'A big blue son of a bitch. The slaughterhouse people took him away.'

5

I have taken the trouble to visit the little train station in which Hazard Lepage awakened: and for my efforts I was molested by a railway dick. The stout gentleman wheezed up to where I was measuring railway ties and informed me, after poking my spine with his cane, that I was trespassing, while in fact I was trying to get some sense of the response our hero must have known when he himself encountered that sudden and alien world.

I entered nevertheless—by persisting—a small white wooden building next to two sets of tracks, and found inside a small green waiting room with a potbellied stove to the right of the door, a pale green bench facing me (a bench with a high, rounded, uncomfortable seat—I asked two ladies to move so I might stretch out upon it), and to my left a canvas stretcher on a rack. With that stretcher two men had carried in Hazard from what was supposedly a carload lot of bones, had placed him on the green bench, his feet towards a roaring fire.

Hazard slowly realized his shoes had been removed; he wondered if he were laid out for burial. Then the brakeman spilled more coffee into his luxuriant beard.

'Where in hell—' Hazard began again.

'No.' The brakeman laughed encouragingly. 'In Edmonton.'

The freight train had whistled blindly in the direction opposite to Hazard's expectations. Instead of being thirty-two miles east of Burkhardt, safe and sound in Coulee Hill with Martha Proudfoot slaving over him, bringing in beer from the beer parlour, a steak from the kitchen—instead of that Hazard was well over a hundred miles west and north of his mansion; and while he travelled for a living, he had not in the past twenty-four years been more than sixty miles from Wildfire Lake. He was frightened, surely; yet when he tried after swallowing a Spam sandwich to sit up and found he had not the strength his only request was 'Put on my damned shoes.'

Hazard was not by nature discourteous. His shoes and over-shoes on, 'Thank you,' he said.

'There's a blizzard blowing,' the brakeman replied. He watched Hazard's dark eyes. He put into Hazard's right hand the second half of the sandwich. 'The slaughterhouse,' he added, 'is east of here along the tracks.'

Hazard, to lift himself upright, let his feet fall off the bench. He asked to be helped to the door; as the door banged open he leaned against the driven snow.

The wind took off his breath. Squinting against the stinging glare, he tried first to keep the bright dazzle of tracks on either side of his invisible overshoes. The measured spacing of ties jarred his knees weak. After what seemed an eternity he became convinced he was walking away from, not towards, Poseidon; he decided to ask again for directions. On turning around, however, he seemed still to be faced into the wind, his cheeks stiff now to the grating snow; he turned again, stumbling: in trying to stand up he tripped across a buried track and smashed himself onto the sill, into the open doorway, of a boxcar: lurching away, scrambling along in the snow, he found not a passageway but another boxcar, and then another, and then still another, and still another. He reached out and caught in his hands what proved to be a steel ladder going up a boxcar's wall. He could not see its top; he let go and turned, the wind catching at his mouth, making him strangle on his own breath. He whirled, falling, stumbled under a car; but as he hesitated on his belly between the two tracks the car or the tracks themselves or he seemed to move: he rolled violently over and was hump-ing his way up from pairs of great iron wheels when he recognized the locomotive on the second set of tracks: a long steel arm punched its way past: he was lost in a blast of steam. Groping.

He struck on the whitewashed fence of a stockyard.

'Posse,' Hazard called. 'Posse! Here, boy!' He crawled up the white plank fence.

Ten or a dozen horses stood dumbly still in the snow dumped

by the wind into the protected pen. They might have been frozen into death, their long hair hardly stirring.

'Poseidon!' Hazard shouted.

An eye blinked dully in a snow-buried face.

Hazard, casting about, recognized now another pen, and beyond it, still another. He hurried as fast as he was able to the second pen, and already beyond the third he could see a fourth; beyond the fourth was a fifth and probably another. And maybe still others.

'Poseidon.' But now he was hardly whispering, strangely responsive himself to the stillness of the horses. Out of the wind he heard the wind. He did not run but walked muffled to the next pen; he called in a muffled voice into the maze of patterned white walls and planks and stilled horses and swirling snow: he did not call but read the horses' colours: dun, pinto, brown. He reached through a heavy gate to brush the snow from a fixed head. Blood gray. He touched a motionless flank. No horse moved. He found under the snow a black roan, a sorrel.

And then in the dizzying white glare he saw—for a moment in the tumble of snow above the dead forms he saw a horse rise, go up, mount: a horse almost white with snow seemed almost to float: and now Hazard was looking for the gate, the animals beginning gently to mill about: 'Poseidon,' a voice was calling.

Hazard found an iron latch: the metal stuck for a moment to his palm. Two hundred horses stirred sleepily towards the open gate. They moved alive, stirred by the man, by the one long creak of an iron hinge, by the urgency of the invisible stallion somewhere in their midst. Hazard could not find a warning shout in his throat: he stepped in front of the leading horse. A black chest did not so much knock him down as brush him into the fluff of snow; he rolled away; he was kicked and knocked flat and he rolled again; and now as he lay on his back in the cushioning snow his knees gone slack the horses leaped at and over him, leaped, went up and over, the shag of winter's bellies went floating up on the choking snow, a very dream of mares: and last, a blue-white, iridescent flash—

26

And with that last flick of a flowing tail or the swung cock of Poseidon himself, a clap of knowing struck Hazard's head: not one but a hundred and a hundred mares: and his for the taking.

In the galloping snow he rose to his knees.

6

Two hours later, Hazard had acquired nothing but an armful of rawhide halters. His ambitions had grown with each failure. Not finding one mare that was adequate to his purpose, he resolved he would have two; and not finding two . . . He had opened gate after gate in vain.

It has been argued that to this day a few wild horses survive in the coulees and ravines of the North Saskatchewan River, there in the heart of the city of Edmonton. At any rate, nearly a thousand horses were in the stockpens the morning of Hazard's arrival, all of them destined for the barrel, can or box: destined to feed the dogs and cats of this fat and ungrateful nation. How many had actually been shot and butchered by noon is undetermined; not more than forty, I would guess.

It was four o'clock in the afternoon when the main herd of nearly eight hundred hit Jasper Avenue at 101st Street; thousands of people were beginning to file into the streets, wondering how best to get home through the drifts piled up by the blizzard. The City Police and the RCMP now recognized the need for immediate action; they began by closing off all exits from the centre of the city: and yet, while they managed to contain the horses, they had not the means by which to capture them. The mayor asked the Army to move in; troops were camped on the Exhibition Grounds; they rolled down Jasper Avenue in armoured troop carriers.

Hazard, forced by his failures to walk, arrived at the Mc-Dougall Church just as the soldiers were abandoning their monstrous vehicles in the streets and adjourning to the nearest beer parlours. He knew that Poseidon, by virtue of living in a house, would not be averse to entering a doorway. For this reason he inquired after his stallion in places like the Rialto Theatre, the Palace of Sweets, and Mike's News-stand. He ducked into Woodward's and asked a girl at the perfume counter if she had seen a big blue stallion come in. 'Only a pair of grays,' the girl replied, pointing to where a floorwalker was cleaning up horse turds with a feather duster: 'They went towards lingerie.' One is tempted to question the sanity of these people. Hazard left immediately and pushed his way into the crowds of horses and shoppers and office workers that thronged the snow-filled streets: the expected reaction of irritation and panic had given way to a mood of jollity and, one must confess, abandon.

Stranded cars were parked every which-way in the drifts; motionless buses and streetcars gave shelter to groups of singing students, to picnicking stenographers who could not find seats in the crowded restaurants. Hazard, entering the Royal George beer parlour, learned that only recently an old racehorse had stopped by and been given two glasses of beer and a dash of tomato juice: 'Have you seen a blue stallion?' Hazard inquired. The men at the table, all of them very drunk (they had been waiting three days to fly to a uranium mine in the North), reported they had seen fleabitten mares, windbroken geldings, a spavined plough-horse, swaybacked saddlehorses. But there wasn't a self-respecting stallion in the bunch.

Hazard, while such concern was being expressed, drank off three glasses from the crowded table—an act which was to discommode him later. He rushed back into the streets: darkness had come, the lights were on. And with darkness, there in the false glare of the gaudy lights, came further chaos.

Liquor rationing was in effect that spring; customers stood in line until they could bear it no longer: then they rioted, carrying off bottles and cases, seizing into their arms what they had so often desired and running wildly into the nearest dark alleys. The clerks made little attempt to stop them; they put aside a bottle here and there—the policemen, of course, were all busy with the horses. 'Pissed to the eyeballs,' was Hazard's way of describing a considerable section of the populace.

Bosses, because they could not get home, were compelled to spend the night caring for secretaries who could not get home (money would hardly buy a hotel room). Soldiers proved willing to occupy the cars that had been abandoned: nor did they suffer the darkness alone, what with many typists and housewives transforming fear into merriment. Only a veil of wind-whipped snow concealed a rash of indecencies. But for a reliable account of what happened as the night wore on I must rely heavily on Hazard's own recollections, and surely in his concern for Poseidon he was likely to overlook details that would be most fascinating to us today. At any rate, his persistence carried him down those long flights of wooden stairs that swoop into the dark river valley. Unknown to himself he explored the haunts of my youth, straying as far west as that lovely forest of spruce that is the city's cemetery (the tree-sifted snow softly burying the stones on which I studied my alphabet). But he stumbled at last on to 109th Street and wandered southward behind a rumour that a number of horses had escaped in that direction.

There is—or at least until this happened there used to be—a statue of a royal lady on a horse on the lawn in front of the beautifully domed Legislative Building. Now a simple cairn has been put up by the Historic Sites and Monuments people, and on it the inscription, 'To this land of prairie, foothill, mountain and river, where the Indian roamed . . .' A group of legislators and a number of women, coming out from an evening session, had surprised Poseidon in the act of confronting his bronze replication.

Hazard, hearing laughter, sought out its source and found his stallion. He must have at that moment known premonitions of a competition that was to enter into his own life. Poseidon snorted in wonder and fear at the poised and perfect bronze beast, approached, turned to lash out viciously with his heels, reared up himself just as the tall bronze stallion reared.

Two strong males contending for one mare could not have been locked into a more desperate equilibrium. Hazard climbed

29

at once on to the ice-sheathed granite base of the work of art, intending to put a halter to Poseidon's head and lead him away in defeat. Instead, he found himself booed and mocked for not letting the battle be resolved.

A man of ministerial voice announced the bronze horse to be superior: 'The artist has done it. In bronze. Forever.'

The man's colleagues repeated these words and nodded: 'Forever. In bronze.' They applauded briefly.

One lady alone was so reckless as to defend the mortal blue stallion against his critics: she praised loudly the fullness of Poseidon's natural endowment, pointing out that the artist, in casting his bronze model somewhat larger than life, had in fact erred in making its parts ridiculously small.

Hazard now in his turn broke into applause. But in doing so he released his firm grip on the bronze stallion's tail: he slipped and fell.

Poor foolish Hazard might have been left lying in the shadows behind the statue had not the same reckless lady become concerned when he did not get up. Indeed, his fall had injured his back—he had all day suffered from the injury he received while struggling to recover his bayonet from the thrashing corpse of what had shortly before been his foe—and only when he tried to sit up and passed out instead was the lady able to persuade the hecklers that the matter was a serious one: she got help from two back-benchers. This was not easily accomplished, for the example of Poseidon . . .

But my story is of Hazard, not of the sordid behaviour of politicians. And Hazard was shortly to betray the intent of his worthy quest. He was to be subverted by the very force in whose name he pretended to act. It was not easy to admit of weaknesses in one's hero: Sir John A. Macdonald tippled, let his biographers quibble as they will; Hazard Lepage was a man of inordinate lust.

When he awoke, to the pressure of two confident hands massaging his spine, he was in the most lavish bed he had ever beheld in his life. It was quite enough to make the seven beds of his mansion look threadbare and worn.

7

He had been carried, under the kind lady's supervision, into the museum. The provincial museum at that time was housed in the Legislative Building. Even today you can ride an elevator to the fifth floor and examine the room, though now it contains the centennial carillon console and a row of twelve chairs. Granted, the Misericordia Hospital is only a few short blocks distant: but on that stormy night the streets were nearly impassable. The lady in question made a snap decision.

She was one of the museum's assistant curators: in that I agree with Hazard. He claimed, however, that her name was Coburne or Cochrane; my own studies lead to a prominent religious family by the name of Cockburn. Hazard recalled that she gave the initial P. as her first name; an affectation I rather applaud, as I expect to sign my own work simply D.—D. Proudfoot. But Hazard described her as a wealthy married woman. The P. Cockburn to whom I located references was single and herself (this strikes one as odd) an artist: she made a specialty of life-sized wax figures, and had made for the museum a number of models of illustrious Albertans.

The room in which he found himself upon regaining consciousness—it was nearly midnight—was an exact replica of the chief factor's bedroom as it existed in the 'Big House', the main residence of the Hudson's Bay post that gave the city its name. The lady, P. Cockburn, explained almost immediately that the Big House had stood exactly where the Legislative Building now stands, a fact which I have been able to corroborate.

You will recall Hazard's peculiar little aversion to the past. He responded by trying to get out of bed.

Getting out of a canopied four-poster which is five feet off the floor is no easy task for a man who is bruised, aching, hungry, suffering from a sore back, and stripped of everything but his socks. Hazard felt very much a prisoner.

The lady, moreover, could hardly be expected to administer to his needs merely by leaning over the sickbed; rather, she must balance precariously on a narrow ladder that had in its middle at least one weak rung. Out of courtesy Hazard signalled her to rest on the bed itself.

She kicked off her shoes rather than stain an historical relic. 'Does that help?' she asked, settling herself on the bed beside him, commencing to massage his sore back.

'It does,' Hazard replied.

She responded to his encouragement.

'A little lower,' Hazard said. 'Yes, there.' And again, 'Yes. There. Just under—' Hazard squirmed away from, then towards her. 'Yes. I have these shooting pains. Ah. Yes. Harder. Harder. Just a little— Gently now.' And then he groaned.

'What is it?' P. inquired solicitously.

He didn't stir.

'I was thinking,' she said. 'While you were asleep and I massaged you.' She brushed her long hair out of his eyes; it commingled with that of his beard. She touched her hands to his hips.

Hazard did not stir.

She touched the undersides of his stiffened knees, his thighs.

'I must make a model of *you*,' she cried out.

Again Hazard groaned.

'Of you,' she insisted. 'In shining wax.'

'My horse,' Hazard whispered. 'Make my horse live.'

That they disagreed is apparent; how they came together is the mystery.

Sexual activity, Hazard swore to me, was the last thing he intended that night. He and P. Cockburn lay together, she naked with him in that great soft nest of a bed, and just as he moved to consummate—her passion, he insisted, not his own—just then, sitting up, kneeling stiffly in the dim light, he was able to see beyond the bed's thin curtains.

Along either side of the high bed were three life-sized figures: on one side the resplendent figure of an Indian chief, the buckskin of an early explorer, the red coat of a North West Mounted

Police constable; on the other the black robe of a missionary, the coat and tails of an early premier, the black gown of a university president.

'Wait a minute,' Hazard cried out. 'Hold on. Who are these pricks?'

Very deftly, P. caught the calves of her legs behind Hazard's knees.

'No,' Hazard said. 'Never. By the humped-up Jesus, I want to get a few things straight. What is this?'

The waxen stares of his audience did not waver, did not diminish. From somewhere overhead a muted light gave shadows to the phlegmatic faces.

'It's not my fault,' Hazard shouted. 'I killed one man in my life. That's all. I was doing my duty.'

The Indian figure wore feathers on its head; the pale feathers, silky, long, torn from an eagle's wing, turned the thin light.

'I was never here before,' Hazard shouted. 'You weren't expecting me.'

Again, no voice, no answer. But the shaping hand of the artist came now to assure his failing courage. And he dared to wrestle.

Hazard did battle: the dear ninny was terrified of history. But in the end and finally, that which he wrestled most was the image of himself for which the hands of P. would seek to take measure. He would not be seduced, he was resolved, into that immortality.

What a shame. We who assemble fragments long for a whole image of the vanished past. We seekers after truth, what do we find: a fingerprint on the corner of a page. A worn step at the turn in the stairway. A square of faded paint on the faded wall. Someone was here, we know. But who? When?

Hazard was determined to take down his salvation with him. And surely, by dawn, he had murdered P. Cockburn's resolve. He gave his foe pleasure until she throbbed dizzy with joy, until she cried aloud a happy 'Hazard!' that set the dark halls to ringing, a 'Hazard!' that must have sent a blush into the cordon of waxen ears. Pity the woman. Pity the poor woman. The artist must hate his creation.

33

B

Old Blue, Hazard explained in his bluff way, by dawn had drowned into the smothering balm of sleep, the distant shore be damned. O that weak stubborn fool, so blind to his larger destiny. 'Did you not,' I cried out to him, dropping my pencil, 'recognize a duty to your fellow beings?' And all he could do was nod and answer: 'I screwed the ass off her.'

8

Martha Proudfoot, at almost that same moment, could talk of nothing but her dear Hazard. I had, only that spring, dropped out of school and left Edmonton; I went to work for Martha's father (my own was killed at Dieppe); Uncle Timothy employed me as a handyman in his hotel there in Coulee Hill.

Because the war was lingering on, help was hard to find. Uncle Tim was more or less laid up with arthritis; Martha was of necessity in charge of the hotel, so she, not my uncle, was my usual companion. And she, it soon developed, was as willing to talk as I was to listen.

Finally, in spite of my innocence, I recognized her basic need and fear: she was terrified that she was in love, not with her remembered fiancé, but with *me*: with the flesh and blood youth who was constantly in her presence—for I helped her to clean tables and to garden and to feed her horses. She dreaded the nature of her response to a vigorous young man of eighteen, and to shore up her crumbling old love (and Hazard was already fifty-one) she must speak constantly of nothing but it. I should have been moved to pity; instead, again in my innocence, I too was becoming responsive to her daily and hourly presence. Not only did we work together; we slept nightly in adjoining rooms, often with neither door locked. Indeed, there was behind my dresser an old door connecting, one might say, our very beds.

But I am mentioning all this to point up an irony. While Martha fought so resolutely to preserve her virginity for that ungrateful

34

man, he, willingly, even thoughtlessly, embraced a woman to whom he was a very stranger. With an almost repulsive bravado he attempted to regale me later with the details of the sordid event.

This P. Cockburn, he announced, was a shade wrung in the withers, which I take it meant she was showing signs of her age and was therefore older than Martha. But, he went on, her tits were like nothing so much as two great speckled eggs of a rare wild bird. And having said this—we were sunning ourselves in rocking chairs on the Eshpeter Ranch—he fell to musing about the eggs of various birds, hoping to find a comparison that might be for me illuminating.

A crow's egg, he guessed first; but no, the colour behind the freckles was lighter. And the freckles themselves: around the nipples they were the shape (very small) and the colour (very light) of the freckles on a chickadee's egg. I confessed that I had never seen a chickadee's egg (though I have gone to some pains since in a vain attempt to find one). But Hazard was unperturbed by my ignorance. Next, farther back from the nipple—he stopped rocking and stared out over the open yard and corrals to the cloud-mottled sky—the freckles were as small and faint as the spots on the egg of a red-winged blackbird. But he shook his head. No, no, larger than that—have you seen a magpie's egg? I had, on one occasion as a boy, gone with two other lads to find the eggs of magpies; we broke into a great stinking nest only to find it was old and deserted and crawling with mites. Finally, Hazard explained, throwing up his hands, there were lovely rich brown spots, like those on a meadowlark's egg. The actual colour of the spots—he turned from the sky to me, intent on refining still further his, shall we say, argument—was the dark boggy brown of the freckles on an oriole's egg. But have you seen the shape, he demanded, the shape of the spots on the egg of one of our own western meadowlarks?

I nodded, simply to acknowledge that I had. One evening as Martha and I walked her mares out past the row of grain elevators and the ball diamond in Coulee Hill, we frightened up a meadowlark, and by the sheerest good fortune happened to find in the long grass its cleverly concealed nest, its three precious eggs. I said nothing of this, naturally, to Hazard, not wanting to upset him; and he by this time had surrendered to his vilest fancies: 'Imagine,' he cried out, 'a great busting pair of boobies the colour of robin's egg blue.'

I was priest to his long confession; and priest also to his erring ways.

Martha's own breasts were of chalk white, their nipples of red jasper. I am sure they were what is called well-preserved, for a woman of thirty-seven, though I have looked upon no others. I have to this day been loyal and faithful to my memories.

But as I say, Hazard was literally swooning in that great luxurious obsolete obscene bed. He awakened to what he thought was the neighing of a horse. A tremor of concern passed through his raw and nearly naked body: for a moment he hankered for yesterday's bed of bones. He raised up on one elbow the better to listen: and only discovered how mighty was his need to relieve himself.

A skylight brightens what was once the museum; stained-glass windows, richly floral in design, turn what might seem a mausoleum into a gently idyllic world. Hazard did not understand the echoes of the word, asylum. The morning light bathed the old museum clean and new. But the poor dear fellow now saw satin bedspreads and the rich patina of oak bedposts as part of his imprisonment. And casting about to find some semblance of a pot, he met again the unwavering stares of his six wax attendants.

Hazard missed the fine complexity of the impending joke: the past which he so scorned was about to save him. At least temporarily.

The North West Mounted Police constable, with a full beard, a scarlet Norfolk-type jacket, white buckskin gauntlets, breeches, boots, and snowshoes, wore especially a hat: a blue pill box, and around it, a white band. Hazard in great haste (impeded by some semblance of an erection) climbed down from the bed, went tip-toe to the constable, and removed the inviting headpiece.

But even Hazard had some little sense of history. He lowered the upturned hat into place. He aimed as best he was able. And yet he could not do what he must.

It was then, while hesitating, he noticed the wonderful dark blue cape with the scarlet lining: slipping first into his own long underwear, Hazard Lepage proceeded to dress as one of Queen Victoria's admirable redcoats.

To his astonishment, the wax figure was complete down to its very belly button and toe nails. Only the male member was disproportionate in size: again, one of my arguments for P. Cockburn's dedication as artist, and for the nature of her guilelessness. Hazard quietly lifted the stiff and open-eyed figure into his place on the high bed, he raised over it the rich old blankets, and P., stirring in her sleep, sighing, snuggled close and slowly moved a hand up the waxen thigh until it rested firmly on the aforementioned member itself.

Hazard had still to urinate. To use his vulgar phrase: his back teeth were floating. He could taste it, he said. His own overshoes in his left hand, the snowshoes in his right, resisting the impulse to touch one farewell kiss to those speckled breasts, he tiptoed out to the circular marble railing that makes of the whole tall building a deep well.

Without further ado he aimed his golden stream at a commemorative garden a number of floors below. That moment was resonant with the future held in store: but Hazard, unthinking, fumbled with the historic buttons, resumed his burden, then went in his cavalier way down the marble stairways, past the rows of glowering oil portraits, past the battle flags to an exit.

A reluctant spring had come to the city. In the east, the sky fanned a small light from the sun's promise. The earth was endlessly white: the roofs, the streets, the parking lots, the snow-bent spruce trees—whiteness everywhere. The sound of a shovel grated in from somewhere distant, digging back to cement and rock and gravel.

Nearer at hand a horse whinnied. Hazard leaned against a Corinthian pillar of Alberta sandstone to put on his shoes;

already he wished he had brought along the redcoat's brown leather belt, the Deane and Adams revolver. He practised a salute with a white gauntlet: only to get tangled in his cape.

Hazard saw his folly. He needed his old green mackinaw and his fur cap: he would turn back: he took in his two hands the great and shining brass knob that would let him change his mind.

The door in closing had locked behind him, had locked him out. He tried again to remember his salute.

9

I too get dressed up: by taking off my clothes. Sometimes of a morning I fold a 3×5 card into a little triangular hat and set it square on my perky fellow's noggin and pirates we sail here together in my bathtub, our cargo the leather-bound books and the yellowing scribblers, the crumbling newspaper clippings and the envelopes with their cancelled stamps and the packs of note-cards that make up the booty of our daring.

What have we captured? what saved?—but the 3×5s speak for themselves:

Into March morning. Hazard commandeers milkwagon.
Bleary-eyed driver voices remorse, disapproval and
indignation that now sweep city at sunrise. Philosophically
asks of Hazard three traditional questions: Why is wickedness
not punished? When? By whom?

I have no record of Hazard's replies. I see it now: perhaps all questions should be answered with questions, as when a smart-alec headshrinker one morning asked me why I did not, sitting in my tub, at least have the decency to take a bath. Was not the Blood warrior, I replied, admired for his ability to endure self-inflicted pain?

I am horny today; horny beyond all containing; wildly horny.

No. Yes, I have quoted correctly. But no date. Why did I not date the card, that I might relish more precisely the exquisite hour of my abandon.

Leads milkhorse and wagon towards corporal who is swinging a lariat. Soldier salutes. Reports he must get to prophylactic station as soon as possible.

Corporal says human skull was found in boxcar full of bones; search is in progress for insane killer who was cornered by police and turned loose hundreds of horses in effort to escape. Hazard expresses concern at seriousness of offence and desires offender might be captured and punished.

Burchard von Oettingen, Landstallmeister of the Royal Stud of Trakehnen: 'Young mares especially are spoiled by too frequent covering.'

Then, strangely, I add a footnote to the same card:

N.B. The scrotum is spoken of as the 'purse'. Investigate implications.

I have arranged the next three cards so as to suggest an order that was not necessarily present in Hazard's rambling conversation:

Second soldier comes through deep snow leading Poseidon by a rope. Hazard feigns interest while soldier speculates: is shocked that any man should wish to kill another. Hazard agrees, putting on snowshoes; amused by distortion of facts he suggests killer must be captured and hanged at public hanging, a fine old custom that must be revived. Both soldiers agree.

Five crows, having circled up from Royal Lawn Bowling Club, fly to lantern that surmounts dome of Legislative Building; Hazard points this out to young men as further sign of advent of spring.

Chase commences; on South Side are Saturday shoppers and farmers in city to see horses. Policeman's version: at Whyte

Avenue pursuers cut off by funeral. Hazard's version: troop movement in early hours; soldiers won't break rank unless commanded. All in new, clean uniforms.

As I reconstruct the event, the milkman was in fact absent when Hazard borrowed the wagon. Some of the streets had been ploughed, but on one side only; thus the milkwagon was stopped in the roadway and the driver, an elderly gentleman, with the earlaps of a fur cap pulled over his ears in spite of the the warming trend, had disappeared limping into a nearby brick house carrying a wire basket full of clinking bottles.

Hazard, I must insist, acted out of good conscience, intending to return the horse as soon as it was feasible; if circumstances were to make this impossible he was hardly to blame. Horses, of course, had an affinity for Hazard. The old chestnut gelding responded to his hand on the bridle; in no time the two of them had disappeared onto the parliament grounds where Hazard met a young corporal and instructed him to hold the milkhorse. Hazard then put on his snowshoes. He walked into a prime stand of spruce below the East Door, and very shortly he stumbled upon a second soldier, a lance-corporal or private who was battling in the deep snow with Poseidon, a lariat around the stallion's neck.

'Let me show you how to do that, young fellow,' Hazard volunteered.

The soldier saluted. In a matter of a few minutes Hazard had fashioned the lariat into a halter: the stallion began to respond to his gentle words and gentler hands. 'You bring up that string of mares,' Hazard now instructed the soldier, indicating a group of mares tethered to the trimmed rows of poplar and elm that make so delightful a colonnade below the Legislative Building.

The soldier saluted; Hazard quietly led Poseidon through the snow and tied him behind the milkwagon. Very shortly the lance-corporal (or private) appeared, leading four captive mares. Hazard tied them to the sides and the rear of the milkwagon.

After taking off his snowshoes and handing them to the corporal who held the milkhorse, he saluted liberally all about, grunting incoherently as he did so.

I wish I could report that all encounters went as smoothly as did this one. Unfortunately, Hazard had to cross the North Saskatchewan River via the High Level Bridge to get onto the road that would take him towards home. And, unfortunately again, the police had by this time got a description of the imagined insane murderer from the brakeman who had laboured to revive the nearly dead body that was Hazard's.

The bridge is a black iron tunnel in which patterns of parallel lines and acute angles are repeated and repeated until they knock at the senses like a film run too slowly: each picture is both separate from and yet like all others. Hazard survived this bludgeoning; then, on the far side of the bridge, at the southern exit where they must angle left and upward and climb a low rise, Poseidon was frightened by a CPR freight train passing overhead on the tracks above the roadway.

My rather extensive investigations into timetables make this exactly 8.44 a.m. Poseidon, in his fright, scared two mares into the narrow lane that was choked with approaching traffic. A truck driver had the courtesy to stop while Hazard tried to calm all his fine collection of horses; they responded by pulling the milkwagon crosswise on the road. The truck driver responded by yelling at Hazard, 'Get that bloody milkwagon out of the way, you little peckerhead.'

'You hangnail pecker yourself,' Hazard replied, throwing off his cape from his red sleeves and his white gauntlets. In his joy at having acquired four excellent mares he became exuberantly reckless. 'Get that roaring truck out of the bloody way and I'll get out of the way myself.'

The driver, a moose of a man, turned off his engine. 'Don't ekerpa me, you pandering redcoat peter,' he shouted back at Hazard.

By this time an appreciative audience of pedestrians, most of them co-eds on their way to the university, had begun to collect;

little did they realize the trucker was offending the very core of Hazard's being.

'You tool,' Hazard said. 'You faltering apparatus.'

'You whang and rod and pud,' the trucker replied.

The girls all together gave a little scream, some of them clapping.

Hazard saw his chance to drive away but missed it in order to shout, 'You dong.' He felt he was coming off rather badly in the exchange. 'You drippy dong. You Johnny and jock.'

The trucker in his excitement was beginning to stutter. 'You diddly dink. You d- you d- you d- you dink. You dick.' I might add that because of this exchange and the consequent delay it occasioned, trucks were forever banned from using the High Level Bridge. 'You dofunny copper,' the trucker added.

Now the group of girls, bright in their green and gold sweaters, jumping up and down, clapping, began to chant: 'Shame. Shame.'

'I'm no damned copper,' Hazard shouted, more to the girls than to the trucker. 'Dohicky to you.'

'Hey,' someone yelled from the cab of another truck. 'You schmucks, both of you get out of the way.'

'You schlongs,' another trucker yelled.

'Shame,' the girls chanted, leaning forward over the rail that kept them off the roadway. 'Shame! Shame!'

But a man in a huge buffaloskin coat and a fur cap, a policeman, was tugging at Hazard's cape. 'Just who are you, sir?' he inquired, gesturing at the same time with a pad of paper he held in his left hand. He had in his right a pencil. 'We have a description, sir, of a short, stocky fellow, a blue bruise in the middle of his forehead—'

Hazard slapped the reins against the milkhorse's flanks, giving out a roar as he did so; the policeman fell out of the way in order to avoid being hit by a wheel.

The chase was on. Hazard galloped his horses through the city streets, yelled at, pursued, condemned, the milkwagon jumping over sidewalks and streetcar tracks, the load of milk bottles spilling out to become white telltale blotches on the snow.

Policemen appeared from nowhere, a pair at this corner, a pair in that doorway. Streets became blind alleys. A track through the snow became a snowbank. 'Stop! Stop him! Stop!' people yelled, standing motionless in swirls of powdered snow. 'Stop that man!' a policeman ordered to a poor chap who had just driven his car into a lamp post. 'Stop him!' two women pleaded when he galloped over their grocery cart behind a Safeway store. But, luckily, Hazard ran into a troop movement. The column of marching soldiers came between him and two dozen pursuers, and the solders, lacking a command, would not break rank. They would not stop.

It was here, however, that Hazard lost two mares; they tore themselves loose in the process of kicking at a vicious dog. The owner of the dog went into a telephone booth to call the police.

Hazard thereafter turned north from the crowds on Whyte Avenue, then drove eastward with new abandon along Saskatchewan Drive and on through a series of sidestreets and back alleys. Survival itself was not impossible, but he recognized he was getting no closer to the Calgary Trail: the road that would take him south to freedom.

He would not escape without Poseidon and his two remaining mares, yet he realized also there was no hope of escaping with them, for he would have again to cross the main thoroughfare. Indeed, he was ready and willing to surrender: but at that moment he could not find anywhere on the white streets a living soul.

Lost and alone in a back alley, he came to what was surely a barn. With no hesitation he stepped from his wagon, opened the barn door, led his sweating gelding inside.

By an act of pure genius he turned loose the last of the mares— as a kind of red herring. He whipped them off down the alley and, certain as death, two policemen appeared on foot from nowhere and ran frantically after the fleeing animals.

Hazard, pleased with his strategy, closed the barn door on Poseidon's heels and collapsed in nervous exhaustion on to an orange crate: only to hear a smaller door creak open in the blank wall against which he leaned. He might in fact have fallen out through the opening door had he not lurched to his feet, grabbed up a pitchfork.

He turned to confront his newest adversary. Poseidon, uneasy in the shadows after the glare of snow, struck out viciously with his head at nothing.

'Easy, boy,' Hazard said.

In at the doorway came a tiny figure. Hazard had remaining in his body just enough strength to knock it into silence. But a kind of hopping chirpiness in the black form made him hesitate. He put down, or, rather, let the fork fall from his hands: it set up a loud clatter in the hollow old building.

'Come,' Hazard said.

His voice echoed back to him: 'Come.'

'Come,' he repeated.

'Come.'

A little old nun in a black shawl came forward to take his hand. She spoke so softly her voice did not echo.

10

Even that first morning, Hazard began to win at rummy. He was smuggled unobtrusively into a big brick building, given a cot behind the furnace, a dish of lukewarm porridge—and then with hardly an introduction he was set in a chair at the card table. They played for an hour before lunch, the five of them, in the furnace room of the Home for Incurables, run by the Sisters of Temperance.

The pipes close over their heads knocked and gurgled. The spiders, after a while, dusted their webs brazenly, waiting for the fat blue flies that buzzed up out of the heat and gloom. The single light bulb strove vainly to belie its forty watts.

Hazard soon learned that there in the furnace room, at a five-sided table, a perpetual game was in progress. He soon learned, also, that none of the other four players could play rummy worth a tinker's damn. Thus it was his winning and yet their insistence that he miss no hand that puzzled him: not only Sister Raphael, but the other players, Miss Boxer and Torbay at first, Stiff later—they would not so much as let him go out to feed his two horses. He was permitted to pay for the oats, but the furnace man went to buy the sacks and to put the feed in the worn feedbox, the water into two scrub pails.

The furnace man himself, deaf and old, never took a hand in the game. The matchbox sitting on a corner of the table was his; each winner dropped in a penny. He worked patiently, shovelling coal and hauling ashes, the furnace door clanking open and shut as he went about his few duties. In the morning the matchbox was always empty; beyond that he seemed to ignore the game, for he could not so much as hear the clinking of coins.

Things were going splendidly for Hazard. He had been happy now since the moment when the little nun, confronting him in what turned out to be an old carriage house, asked shyly, gently: 'Do you play cards?' Since nodding in the affirmative he had accumulated in addition to the cost of oats and a few bales of hay, twenty-five dollars; not to mention receiving a warm bed free of charge for four nights, enough to eat daily for five consecutive days. He could already feel just the slightest paunch under his constable's uniform.

It was a faint sense of boredom at forever winning that got him into his first real trouble: on the evening of the fifth day Torbay won the only hand he had won in a day and a half. Let me add that this Torbay was an old fool who to me, as you shall recognize, was a considerable embarrassment; I say this in spite of having been told that in his youth he was the handsomest man in all of Ontario.

Hazard threw in his own hand, face down.

Torbay, instead of picking up the cards so that he might proceed to deal, turned to Sister Raphael: 'I rise to Point of Order.'

'Thank you, Torbay,' Sister Raphael said. 'Please state the Point of Order.'

'Our Visitor must cast in his cards face up.'

It so happened that on this particular evening—it was 8.44 pm and past official bedtime—all the players were present and playing. This was seldom the case. Hazard marvelled again at the nun's authority, for while she was over eighty she was certainly the youngest of the group.

She nodded firmly, as did the other players.

On Hazard's left at the pentagonal table sat the indignant Torbay, a long wraith of a man. Next to Torbay sat Sister Raphael. On Hazard's right sat Stiff, hunched forward over his knuckles and cards, and behind Stiff, Hole, who never played but only watched: the couple were, in defiance of their advanced years, outrageously indecent in their show of affection for each other— indeed Hole would go so far as to aggravate Stiff during the game by fingering his fly. Then, on Stiff's right, sat an extremely old lady, Miss Boxer, who, when she spoke at all, spoke only of her elaborate plan to visit the Old Country one more time before, as she put it, she went to meet her Maker.

Hazard gave a chuckle and turned up his hand for in fact he had, perhaps out of a sense of shame in addition to his growing boredom, sat for two rounds holding a winning hand. 'You caught me with my finger on the trigger,' he announced ever so glibly.

Torbay glared, not at Hazard, but at Sister Raphael: 'I move that our Visitor be expelled this evening from the Home for Incurables.'

Hole, who was given to kibitzing, touched carefully with a middle finger the dried matter from the corner of each eye, then broke in: 'Now he's as bad as the rest of you. He tries to cheat—'

'Out of order,' Sister Raphael interrupted. 'Does anyone second the motion?'

A long pause ensued: it may well have lasted as many as five minutes. Sister Raphael, obviously, hoped the motion might not find a seconder, for she enjoyed Hazard's presence as much as did ladies of more dishonourable intent. Hazard himself for a moment imagined spending five dollars on his drive home; thus he would be left with twenty dollars with which to buy George Campbell's one last mare. But to his own surprise he turned on Torbay: 'You don't even *try* to win, Torbay. You pick up the wrong card. You throw away cards I need. Damnit, man, this isn't a game at all. I haven't got a chance. I haven't got a ghost of a chance. What is this?'

'It is my motion,' Torbay said. 'I speak first.'

'Speak,' Sister Raphael said, a chirpy little fire of impatience coming into her calcined blue eyes.

'I would suppose,' Torbay said, 'that ninety-nine decimal nine years of responsible existence are to count for something on this earth. Surely as the oldest surviving member of the Proudfoot family—'

'Proudfoot!' Hazard burst out.

'Indeed, my young pipsqueak,' Torbay said. 'None other. The same.'

'Do you know the Proudfoots of Coulee Hill by any chance?'

'I have the misfortune to be related to that bad lot.' Torbay nodded vigorously. 'Tad Proudfoot is so crooked he must screw his socks on. Titus is dead on the beaches of Dieppe, I am told, and thanks be to a generous God. Timothy Proudfoot, who once beat me out of a pregnant mare and a new saddle, is the worst horse thief in the country. He has a thriving hotel and livery barn to prove it.'

Hazard was somewhat taken aback; the future father-in-law of his acquaintance was a grouchy dull slow man who had arthritis, two fine automobiles that he washed weekly, and an endless supply of coupons for rationed gasoline. 'His daughter Martha,' Hazard replied irrationally, 'has five of the finest Arab mares in this part of the world.'

'I am speaking,' Torbay said, 'of the Proudfoots of Coulee Hill—'

'Gentlemen,' Sister Raphael interrupted again, 'we have a motion before us. I do not recall its being seconded.'

Hole had been whispering feverishly into the nun's good ear.

'This pipsqueak comes in here,' Torbay said, 'and we offer him our hospitality. Now he has not the courtesy to win what he wins. In all my mortal existence I never—'

'Never what?' Hole taunted.

'Never you mind never what,' Torbay said. 'You left your pants off again today.'

At this remark Stiff could no longer remain silent: 'Miss Boxer is going to report you to the Sister Superior if you follow her up to her ward again.'

'Why should I *follow* Miss Boxer, pray tell? She is a lady in every way, are you not, Miss Boxer?'

Miss Boxer, searching in her sleeve for a handkerchief, found herself too modest to reply.

'There,' Torbay said.

But Hole would not leave him alone. She rolled her eyes suggestively, then fluttered her orange lashes. And she began a taunting chant: 'Someone has a bone-on. Someone has a bone-on. Someone has a bone-on.'

Torbay's pale, long face flushed a blood red.

'O Sister Raphael,' Miss Boxer cried softly, her toothless 'O' of a smile dimly afloat in a puddle of rouge, dark beneath a silky moustache. 'I do wish you had your encyclopaedia now.' This remark each of the players addressed at least once a day to Sister Raphael, who on hearing it each time modestly blew her nose. 'At least,' Miss Boxer went on, 'in the Old Country we had our books.'

'No one,' Sister Raphael insisted, dabbing at the tip of her rather stubby nose with a green handkerchief, 'has seconded the motion. So let us go on—'

But just then Stiff said, 'I second the motion.'

Hole delivered a vicious jab to his ribs; in reacting he bit his tongue.

Sister Raphael picked up the deck—she seemed about to deal—then peevishly she slapped it down in the middle of the table. 'By voice count.'

Torbay spilled his huge hands like a bowl of sausages from his lap on to the table. 'Ladies and gentlemen,' he began, his voice infinitely weary, 'again I must act as your conscience. You well know that while I may have little in the way of worldly possessions, I have never cheated at cards.' He stuck out his gray tongue at Hole, who leaned forward across Stiff's shoulder. 'I have never sullied my body with sexual indulgence.' Here he nodded his dried head down at his lap. 'I am reminded of a momentous occasion by Our Visitor's scarlet tunic and by the horses that accompany him. Let me explain once more by way of preamble that my brother and I came West as blacksmiths—farriers, to be precise—and were present on that fateful 16 November in 1885 in Regina when Louis Riel was hanged by the neck. My brother left our places of honour resolved to marry: he did so within six weeks, he fornicated his way into an early grave and since has lost one of his despicable sons who rather than support me in what they chose to call my dotage, confined me to this institution in the Year of Our Lord 1921, disturbed as they were by the rise in the price of flour—'

'That was the year I found my first horse,' Hazard broke in. 'Twenty-four years ago this very—'

Sister Raphael winked at him, then added sternly: 'Order please.'

'My dear pipsqueak,' Torbay went on. 'Hanging would be too good for you. The world is much too full of horses. Their stink is forever in the streets of the city, as I too well recall. But to continue, I too made a resolve on witnessing the untimely end—'

'Next,' Sister Raphael interrupted.

Stiff in turn folded his long white hands into a heap of silvery knuckles in the middle of the table; his fingers could barely find an edge whereby to lift a card, with the result that the sometimes extremely long delay had more than once irritated Hazard. 'Ladies and gentlemen, I seconded the motion. I am not one given to supporting the moral censures of Mr Proudfoot; but this lady'— he nodded over his left shoulder, thus bumping noses with Hole and getting some of her orange powder onto his own—'and I like to feel that we have found here a home—'

'Of course,' Sister Raphael said. 'Next, please.'

Miss Boxer sighed a tremulous sigh that Hazard hoped might be meant for him. Her cracked and painted nails fluttered like dying butterflies onto the table. 'In the Old Country, men are handsome beyond all description. Integrity is the mark of a gentleman. Should I win, then, enough at our harmless little game, I propose most surely to return to a very fine person who waits even now . . . '

'I am sorry,' Sister Raphael said abruptly. 'Three affirmative votes. Cut the deck, please.'

Miss Boxer, dazed, remembering the disconsolate lover who awaited her return, stirred but slowly, reluctantly reached out and cut the deck.

'Whorehouse cut,' Torbay insisted.

Miss Boxer made the double cut, then turned up the top card.

Sister Raphael, her calcined blue eyes sad, even pained, turned her gaze from the card itself—it was the five of hearts—to Hazard's watching face. Had she not drawn dark eyebrows on to her high forehead, she might have been genuinely beautiful. 'You should leave us now, Our Visitor. But of course the choice is difficult—'

Torbay and Stiff closed their eyes as if they might be praying. Hazard put his hands on the table. As he stared out over the watching eyes of the women he chanced to notice that a spider, working industriously, skilfully, had fashioned a web between an upright timber of the coalbin and the back of Miss Boxer's head. Sister Raphael, turning the emerald ring on the little finger of her right hand, continued in a voice that was nearly the drone of drowsing bees:

'And necessarily so. We have, after all, five fingers on each hand. Our language is host to five vowels. We have each of us five senses.'

Hazard nodded.

'We once met an Indian,' the nun continued, 'who recognized five points to the compass: east, south, west, north, and centre. A fine distinction. And is not the wild rose of Alberta five-petalled?'

'It is,' Hazard said. 'I have while travelling many times gathered a pocketful of orange-red hips and nibbled them at my leisure.'

Now it was the nun who nodded. 'You should by all rights leave,' she insisted again.

Torbay opened his eyes and picked up the deck and dealt four cards around the table.

'Please,' Hazard said. 'Please.' He dropped a coin into the matchbox. 'I apologize. I won't lose again. Deal me in.'

I I

Stretched out on his cot behind the furnace that night, snug and cozy, his feet and shoes on an old copy of *Maclean's*, Hazard wondered for a long time about the Englishman who had refused to leave the mansion on the cliff overlooking Wildfire Lake. When Derek Hardwick was informed in 1918 that the Great War was over, he refused to believe it. Rather, he decided the German Army had instigated a plot aimed at making him surrender his fort, and that he would not do. He would not be deceived into being captured. So he loaded his three shotguns, hauled coal and wood and food—winter was pressing hard upon him—into his mansion, and he prepared to make his last stand. He had completed the mansion on the day Queen Victoria died; he would himself die rather than surrender, for he intended to keep everything intact as it was on the day of its completion.

But no one attacked the doughty warrior. And when, finally, a curious neighbour had not seen the old man around for a few days and ventured within shotgun range, no shots were fired. The neighbour went and got a friend and the two of them, in a good stout wagon box, drove closer.

Derek Hardwick was dead in the cellar: he had been digging a well through his cellar floor, lest his cistern go dry, apparently, and he had slipped into the well and drowned.

There are two versions of what happened next. Some say the corpse, because of its odour, was simply buried where it floated. Others say it was cremated and the ashes sent back to the moors of Yorkshire. At any rate, the cellar was sealed off and Hazard never opened it.

Thinking, dozing, he recognized old Hardwick's folly. Why, then, he wondered, why should he himself venture outside the Home for Incurables and return to that mansion? At the mansion he was alone; here he had company. There he must care for his horses; here it was done for him. And all he had to do was go on winning and winning and winning.

In spite of his growing concern, he must have fallen asleep, for the next thing he knew Sister Raphael was gently shaking him awake. He opened his eyes to a steaming hot pot of coffee, to buttered toast with jam and a bowl of oatmeal that was running over with milk and brown sugar. 'Come, come,' the old nun said, and tugged her black shawl about her shoulders.

But this morning she did not hurry away; rather she sat down on an orange crate, carefully lifting her skirts away from the ashes and dust on the disintegrating cement floor, raising her button shoes on to a block of wood. She watched him as he dipped a large and ornate silver spoon into the oatmeal; then of a sudden she burst out, 'May I pray for you?'

Hazard laughed, shaking his head, dipping a thick slice of toast into the steaming cup of coffee even as she poured it. 'I have nothing left to pray for.'

'Then why do you wish to find the mare?'

The tiny old sister spoke with something of an accent (though Hazard could never establish its origin), and now he did not quite understand her:

'*La mer*?' he said.

'The mare,' she repeated. 'The mare. Why do you wish—'

Hazard had not mentioned his quest to anyone in the Home. He spread whole strawberries out of the dish of jam on to a slice of toast. 'Nobody said I do.' He was irked by the question. 'I wish you had your encyclopaedia now, Sister Rafe. I don't understand—'

But while he spoke Sister Raphael winked; and just as she winked he got his idea.

'Boredom,' he said, to cover his excitement.

'Boredom?' the nun asked.

'Boredom,' Hazard said. 'Straight stinking boredom. Win win win win win. I'm human too, you know.'

He had hurt the good sister's feelings; at the very moment when he conceived his plan for doing her a favour. She did not wait for the empty dishes but politely excused herself and slipped away into the shadows.

That night, on the pretext of going to take a much-needed bath in the furnace man's bathroom, Hazard found access to a telephone. He called a small second-hand bookstore that used to stand where the Macdonald Hotel now rises: I believe it was called the Oxford and Cambridge Bookstore. Yes, the owner had an old set of the *Encyclopaedia Britannica*. 'Hold it until I show up,' Hazard said. 'The name please?' the voice asked. Hazard feared that his own name might have been discovered and would be recognized. 'Proudfoot,' he said.

But Hazard did not that night go for the books. He waited until all had retired to their rooms or wards, until the furnace man himself had dozed off at the card table—and then he could not find the strength that would enable him to sneak out.

Three or four days elapsed in quick succession. Now he had forty dollars and one cent. Much of the money was in small coins; on the night he passed the forty-dollar mark he rummaged in the coalbin and found a discarded boot. And as he was counting nickels and dimes and quarters into the boot he heard footsteps echoing towards him. He looked around from his preoccupation.

Torbay, in a long gray nightshirt, came trailing and ducking (no end of pipes angled close above Hazard's cot) into the small ring of light. Torbay was nervous, uneasy; he slumped onto the orange crate. He studied for a long while the calendar over Hazard's bed: the fly-specked calendar with its picture of a full-rigged sailing ship was twenty-four years out of date and had fooled Hazard badly until he happened to notice his misreading.

'Counting your winnings I see,' Torbay ventured, trying to make a little joke.

Hazard did not deign to reply. As a matter of fact, he had commenced to count his coins with an intrusive regularity. Scratching with a sharp nail he had made of a length of 2×4 a kind of ledger; under the five headings 1, 5, 10, 25 and 50 he made a mark for each coin, four upright or vertical scratches being joined or bisected by one horizontal mark to signify a total of five. But this method of reckoning must constantly be checked against the actual accumulation of money.

Torbay, finding that his humour fell on deaf ears, tried another tack. 'I've been dying to ask you,' he said, 'since you represent'—and he could not resist a note of sarcasm—'the eternal violence of law and order—'

'When am I leaving?'

'Not quite—'

'Why am I staying?'

'Aha. But not that either.' Torbay shook his head; even in the fragility of his age it was apparent he had once been exceptionally handsome. 'Tell me, good man. Would you settle for a lump sum?'

Hazard couldn't resist a smile. 'You're pulling my leg.'

'Name your price. Anything.'

'You're like the rest of us, Torbay. You haven't got a pot to piss in.'

'Those who keep track of my money tell me I'm a millionaire.'

'That's ridiculous,' Hazard said. But, using his fingers, he combed his hair.

Torbay squinted, bending in at the top of Hazard's bootful of coins. His voice came muffled: 'You have a lot then yourself?'

'Well, not a great lot—' Hazard pushed his 2×4 under the cot.

Torbay shook his head, the white hair that flowed over his shoulders giving off the sweet odour of talcum powder as he did so. 'Please, please,' he burst out. 'Just don't take me away.'

'Who said I was leaving?' Hazard shouted. 'Who the hell said I was leaving?'

'I'll pay any price,' Torbay pleaded. He straightened stiff on the orange crate. He pressed his nightshirt to his thighs. 'Please,' he begged, rising now as if to be led away.

'Sit down,' Hazard said. 'Let's not lose our self-control. We can talk about this like rational men.'

Torbay crossed his wrists, as if tied, over his private parts. '*Please*,' he pleaded one more time. 'Don't blame me. I'm no different.' His old voice tightened almost to a shriek. 'I goddamned well want to live forever too.'

'No!' Hazard shouted.

But Torbay was gone.

'No! No! No!' Hazard leaped up from the cot to seize the old man. He followed the sound of Torbay's feet into a dark hallway through a low door into another and darker hallway and into another room and still another, and then another, each smaller, each darker: into a large low-ceilinged room that was surely the laundry. 'No!' Hazard shouted into the shadowed darkness. He stopped dead still between two rows of what appeared to be drying sheets. The air was damp to his face. And now he heard a voice.

A woman giggled softly, as if smothering in the very darkness; it was the unmistakable giggle of Hole. Hazard, in acute embarrassment, turned to sneak away, only to tumble headlong into a pile of dirty bedclothes. He lay tangled and gasping, trying not to inhale the odours of sweat and vomit and excrement. But the voice of Stiff was soft and caressing above his own hard breathing: 'Your breasts,' he was saying so lovingly in the angled shadows, 'are like the great speckled—'

Hazard leaped up and was gone from the room in one bound. He dashed at a shadow he assumed to be a second door: only to be slapped across the face. He seized wildly at the tall figure that blocked his way.

He found, touching gingerly here and there, he had caught instead of Torbay a suit on a hanger.

And there in the dark, on an impulse, Hazard traded his constable's bright uniform for the clothes he could not see. He put on the trousers, the old-fashioned collar, the coat: and all proved to be a perfect fit. He secured the fly and picked up his shoes; and walking in his stockinged feet he felt his way with his free hand from wall to wall, not trusting a crack of light under a door, the pattern of shadow askew on a doorjamb.

Back in the furnace room beside the cot, Hazard found to his surprise he was dressed as a clergyman. He brushed his new suit clean of ashes, put water on his hair, picked up his bootful of coins, and carefully he stole outside.

Only now did he put on his own shoes. He found the door to the carriage house unlocked; he found one set of harness; within a few minutes he drove out into the alley with his gelding and milk-wagon.

It was a warming if not a warm night. The gelding was obviously glad to be away from the unruly stallion. The streets were clear of snow; the sky was a purple umbrella over the city. Hazard had only once to ask directions, of a lady out walking a dog; in a short while he stopped in front of the bookstore. The owner at that moment was pulling down the blinds.

The set of Encylopaedias proved to be valued at twenty-nine dollars. The elderly bookseller, limping somewhat, assisted by his wife, helped Hazard load the twenty-nine blue-bound volumes into the milk-wagon. Hazard didn't have the heart to quibble about the price; he was being accorded the deference due a man of God. He carried his bootful of money into the store and counted out neat piles of coins onto a high oak counter, putting only nickels on nickels, dimes on dimes, and so on.

'Will there be anything else, Mr Proudfoot?' the bookseller asked, counting coins off the piles as rapidly as Hazard arranged them.

Hazard made some pretence of examining a Bible—it proved to be printed in German. Reluctantly he demolished the stacks of coins the bookseller had not claimed, filling the right pocket of his black suitcoat with dimes, the left pocket with quarters.

'Your boot, Mr Proudfoot,' the bookseller said as Hazard fiddled with the key of the locked door.

'Not at all,' Hazard replied.

The bookseller eyed both Hazard and the empty work-boot

with growing misgivings. He picked up the boot, then put it down. 'Mr Proud—'

Hazard, pulling with both hands, jerked the knob off the door.

The two men were quite at a loss as to how they might get out of the room. The bookseller's wife put on her glasses. Fortunately for all concerned, a policeman on his beat heard the racket inside: using the outside knob he opened the door, striking Hazard across the nose in the process. The policeman was wearing a buffaloskin coat. Both he and Hazard apologized to each other. The bookseller apologized to both men, then to his wife, who took off her glasses.

Hazard's drive back to the Home was uneventful, except that he began to realize the milk-wagon stank atrociously of spilled milk and cream. When he got to the carriage house, finding everything normal, he turned on one small light and took away from Poseidon's head a scrub pail full of water.

While moving the books out of the milk-wagon he chanced to pick up the thirteenth volume last. 'HAR to HUR' he read on its spine. Out of curiosity he opened the volume: HARMONY to HURSTMONCEAUX.' The latter word, especially, caught his attention. HARMONY . . . no . . . HEAVEN . . .

Page 712: HORSE: *Equus caballus*: anatomy . . . size and stride . . . elegant shape . . . powers of endurance . . .

And he read now, stumbling over a fork handle as he looked for a seat, squatting onto an orange crate: 'The points of chief importance are a fine, clean, lean head, set on free from collar heaviness; a long and strongly muscular neck, shoulders oblique and covered with muscle; high, long withers, chest of good depth and narrow but not extremely so; body round in type; back rib well down; depth of withers a little under half the height; length equal to the height at withers and croup; loins level and muscular; croup long, rather level; tail set on high and carried gracefully; the hind quarters long, strongly developed, and full of muscle and driving power; the limbs clean-cut and sinewy, possessing abundance of good bone—'

Hazard slapped the book shut: 'No. Not ever again. Never.'

He slammed down the book on the floor beside the others. He went into the darkness at Poseidon's head and spoke into the stallion's ears and eyes, into his very teeth. 'No! You four-legged cock! No!'

And he explained, yes: his own predicament, the horse be damned: he had travelled bent and freezing against the snows of spring and now he was warm; rain squalls came with thunder to drive him across a treeless prairie and now he was dry; hail-storms knocked at his eyes and set the cannonballs of ice to leaping on the sun-packed roads; mud spattered him brown and gritty black; the wind drove dust into his flesh.

He had slept in haylofts, he explained, in bunkhouses and granaries and strawpile bottoms. He ate leftovers at kitchen tables when gangs of men had finished eating; he made do on stale sandwiches brought back from hay meadows, on yesterday's fly-touched dessert. He got up in darkness, startling mice away from the warmth of his body, and he led his prick of a beast of a stallion to breed mares before they went into the fields to pull a drill or a harrow or a plough. He drove hard to get to another farm by noon, when the teams came in from the fields to eat and rest. He drove all afternoon and sometimes into the night, then rounded up likely mares out of a pasture. He was the man from whom each farm must have its visits; yet he must eat alone, travel alone, work alone, suffer alone, laugh alone, bitch alone, bleed alone, piss alone, sing alone, dream alone—

And his voice echoed back in the empty carriage house:
'No!'
'No,' he said. 'Stop it. Stop!'
And 'Stop!' came the echo.

12

He led them out of the doorway, into the alley, the gelding strain-ing against the traces. The halter rope came tight at the back of the wagon; then the pressure was gone and Hazard knew the stallion was following. The gelding, the bearded man in the black suit, the milk-wagon, the lovely blue stallion—they moved from the alley and into the traffic, moved into the kniving blaze of lights, the blare of a horn. A bus swerved to avoid Poseidon's rear end. The gelding broke into a milk-horse trot.

They escaped unnoticed onto the Calgary Trail; and Hazard did not once look back at the glow on the sky, at the crescent of lights that offered a bright embrace. Rather, looking forward into the dark, into the silence, he made out the glaze of snow that temporarily covered the stubble fields, the fences that squared the rugged land.

He had impetuously flung himself from the arms of sane comfort, even a kind of luxury, into the whoreson workaday world. And his only means of livelihood was the white and black dink of that stallion.

A treacherous fate; a treacherous fate, indeed. Three dollars per jump; ten dollars per standing colt—if he found a mare to be put to the horse. A preposterous fate, to be at the mercy of something so rash, so reckless and fickle, so wilful, unpredictable, stubborn—and so without morality. The organ of copulation of a horse is of a three-part structure not unlike the contemporary spaceship; a kind of trinity of woe.*

I myself prefer an ordered world, even if I must order it through a posture of madness. It is the only sane answer to prevailing circumstances. I live amply off my nasty rich relatives who are embarrassed that I so much as exist. Because of their hypocrisy and pride and shame I am able to live regally. Special

* For an excellent illustration of the penis of the horse, see *The Horse Its Treatment in Health and Disease*, Prof. J. Wortley Axe, M.R.C.V.S., editor, 9 volumes (London, The Gresham Publishing Company, 1905–06). See especially Volume IV, p. 69, for: 1. Transverse Section of Penis, 2. Longitudinal Section of Glans Penis, 3. Penis unsheathed. I have here in my bathtub with me the complete set, bound in the original decadent green covers; a set I felt free to acquire by stealth from a local university due to the general neglect accorded hippological studies in the modern centre of learning.

treatment in this institution costs a pretty penny indeed. I eat better, I dress better (when I choose to dress) than the wealthiest of my blood relations. Amply, I indulge myself. And I have not worked a day of my life since that fateful summer of 1945. Because, you see, I prefer my studies and my privacy.

Yes, dear reader, I am by profession quite out of my mind. And I recommend it heartily to anyone who has courage, genuine integrity, an appetite for evening walks in the country, a tolerance of variety in one's fellow humans, a capacity to entertain leisure at infinite length. And I dare tell you this because I know your passion for dull blinding labour and hollow success will keep you from crowding me out of my sinecure.

I would certainly have finished my life in absolute content-ment, had I not recognized my obligation to complete this infernal biography: Hazard was on the road again, the road leads to those long straight parallel sets of tracks that go it would appear from nowhere to the blank horizon.

For four days he wandered a free man, stopping to cook a modest meal over a fire by the roadside, driving on in the spring sunshine, stopping at ugly little filling station-restaurants for coffee and gossip, sleeping at night in his milk-wagon in the shelter of a poplar grove or a strawpile. He was able, for four days, to pretend his gipsy existence was, in itself, enough and sufficient. On the fourth day, however, he found what surely he had been seeking all the time: he found a mare in heat.

I say heat because Hazard himself never used the expression, oestrus. He had first turned off the highway looking for a road that would be easy on his horses' feet (and the stallion he dis-covered had been freshly shod while at the Home for Incurables). Then from gravel he went to a dirt road. That he did not proceed directly towards Coulee Hill and his beloved Martha I explain as follows: he thought of the horses in the little sawmills, on the Indian reservations south and west of the city. Thus he strayed on to a loggers' trail and into the bush country west of his destination. And surely the glare of the sun on snow that had melted in the wheat fields, only to freeze again, was enough to make him seek comfort in the forest: the confrontation with mere space can be so appalling. As a result of all this he wound up quite by chance in a little resort town on a lake which I shall refrain from naming: many of you have swum where Poseidon freely relieved himself, for he was always a torrential pisser, a virtue, incidentally, which as you shall presently learn is never to be sneezed at.

On 23 March the town was very nearly deserted; the silence, the stillness of summer ghosts, hung in the tall spruce and the bare poplar and birch along the absolutely deserted beach. The lake was ice-bound, the ice covered with snow. The field of white was quite intense enough to obliterate the tracks and stains and boxes left by an occasional ice fisherman. Far distant across the lake, above the low line of hills, the sky was by contrast a deep and horsy blue.

One of the summer ghosts must surely have been mine. I know that lake only too well, for as a child I had my first encounter with cousin Martha on its sandy shores. Hazard, of course, could know none of this: he led his stallion into town, looking for an open grocery store where he might spend one or two of his remaining eight dollars—and accidentally he strayed upon a riding stable.

It was mid-afternoon; the town's few inhabitants were asleep. Spring, one street in from the colder beach, had set eaves to dripping with the regularity of a thousand metronomes. The sun was cruelly bright. The corral outside the riding stable gave some slight shelter to eight or ten horses and two ponies: and most of them were mares.

Even from a considerable distance Hazard saw one mare prick up her ears when Poseidon whinnied; Poseidon, for the first time in four days, resisted his halter rope and the leader rein that Hazard had fashioned of a broken set of snow chains. Hazard, perhaps out of habit, investigated: one mare was indeed in full heat—unfortunately she had a neck that was too long and a head too large. A second and younger mare was creamy white and beautifully formed: unfortunately, she was pretty much gone out of season.

Just as Boreas, the north wind, did not scruple to mate with untended mares, so Hazard on impulse decided to service free of charge the unattended younger animal. He had no difficulty in putting ropes to the halters the mares already wore. And to further his run of good luck, he found a high fence, a long pole, and a patch of sloping ground behind a summer cabin that bore the unlikely name, Weehafun.

Here I must become technical. Sometimes a stallion will not respond to a mare that is going out of heat; he will not rise to a mare that simply does not get very hot. And a mare not in full heat—a cranky mare, as the expression has it—will kick back in a dangerous fashion at the sniffing and biting, the reckless pawing, the trial and futile jumps that are essential to the final consummation: the stallion to retaliate ignores her. But by a procedure known as teazing (I prefer the archaic spelling), a mare in full heat is used to get the stallion ready; then, upon being aroused, he is content to mount the mare not of his first choice.

I have mentioned that Hazard and Martha were approaching the fourteenth year of their engagement. Let me go back to the ninth for a moment: in the summer of that year my parents and I were staying in a large log cabin on that same lake: Hazard and Martha came on a Sunday with Martha's father (he was long a widower) to pay us a visit. My Uncle Tad happened to drop in also: the four men got into a horseshoe game which it seemed would never end.

The horseshoes soared all afternoon, glinting in the afternoon sun as they curled upward, clanking of a sudden onto an iron post. The four men laughed and opened more bottles of beer; they picked up each in turn another pair of shoes; each in turn took careful aim through the upraised but broken circle, stepped forward, swinging an arm, letting go; each hestitated, the pose unbroken, watching in pure delight and fearful anticipation.

Towards evening Martha tired of counting ringers and leaners and sliders; she realized she would never go in swimming if she waited on those four men; she donned her swimsuit and holding my hand took me for a long walk down the beach. When finally she decided to enter the water I sat on the beach digging a hole in the sand, watching the water seep up slowly to fill it. While I have never been sick a day in my life, I believe I did at the time have a mild sunburn; at any rate I was never extremely fond of water.

Martha was gone for so long that after a while, tiring of my castle building and moat digging, I retired to the trunk of a rather tall spruce where I might lean in comfort under the spreading boughs and at my leisure watch the not undistinguished sunset. It was becoming quite dark; I began to fear Martha had forgotten or deserted me. You must walk out very far to get to deep water; she might have returned to the cabin by another way . . .

But then, to my great relief, she appeared from the threatening darkness: alone, humming to herself, she emerged on to the completely deserted beach as if coming out of the set sun. You must join me in imagining what I saw: she was as naked as the lake's surface itself. While out swimming she had on impulse stripped off her suit, and now she carried it casually in her left hand. It was that cooling hour when the water is at its warmest. But surely she knew I could see, even in the lake's twilight, her glistening full breasts, her pubic hair a great slick patch of honeyed seaweed dripping water from each wisp and curl. Then she stopped at the water's edge to raise a foot in one hand and brush off the shell of a tiny dead clam. She stopped directly before my gaze to rinse at the water's edge the sand from her naked feet, intending at first, I trust, to step into her sandals.

I lay in the shadows of a large spruce. She pretended not to see me as she touched her own soft body with curious hands; she cupped a tipped breast as if to taunt the broken circle of the moon; she brushed the clinging drops of water from the round perfection of her belly; she bent and scooped in her soft white palm a sweep of water and gushed it into the private shadows of her naked body. Surely she knew I was watching—and in the assurance of her beauty she put down her bathing suit on her beach sandals, picked up a huge blue towel, and there in the last red glow of my long vespers she rubbed her taut skin warm;

she towelled and smoothly massaged the mould of her long and creamy thighs, her swelling hips and buttocks and the nest of hair—

Dear God, even now, thinking, I remember my own fumbling haste in the presence of her calm disregard. There in the gum-scented shadows my own body, itself scented warm, responded rudely to hers—there beneath that dark and bleeding spruce, the stillness redolent with the saskatoon berries I had idly crushed to my lips, my hand responded to my hard longing. You must have heard the little joke about how one might go crazy; but in the shelter of the growing darkness, all my senses sane and alive—there, caught in the fury of my own fist, I gave unwittingly a soft groan at my savage pleasure—or was it pain? Martha turned with a start, not towards me, but towards the water. Softly she called, as if I must protect her against the night: 'Demeter?'

Forgive my misfortune—my dear mother, pretending to know-ledge and believing Demeter to be a masculine name, affixed it to my birth certificate.

'Demeter?' Martha called again.

I could find no voice to answer with. My very wanting had choked me into silence.

13

But I was explaining Hazard's predicament. He constructed a makeshift snorting pole against the high fence and led the hot old mare head foremost into the V. Then he led the stallion alongside, protected by the pole from unexpected kicks. But the mare was on and did anything but resist; she might have been covered that instant. Who was teazing whom was never in doubt. Poseidon could not long remain indifferent to the apparent opportunity; in a few minutes he began biting at her head, moving down her long neck towards her sweating flanks. Both of them squealed now in the bestiality of their lust; the old mare rubbed against the pole, trying to swing under the stallion's jump; the stallion trembled, greedy for joy. Now Hazard was able to apply a handful of olive oil (his first purchase on leaving Edmonton) to the stallion's member. But still the young mare, tethered nearby, was slow to commence her hunching and urinating. Hazard, using his own right hand and arm, checked to see if she was beginning to flush and open. Then, encouraged, holding the halter rope and leader rein, he swung Poseidon of a sudden towards the virgin mare.

Poseidon, his mouth foaming, bit cruelly at the young mare's neck, tearing the skin clean of hair. But now the mare did not cringe away. The great blue beast rose along the virgin's white side, on to her back, his iron shoes striking blood from her flanks; but this time she braced her forelegs and swung sideways under him. Hazard had discreetly found a slight rise on which to place her front hoofs. He held the stallion's head by the long chain; with his right hand he whisked the mare's tail aside and guided the precious cock on its dark voyage; to save time, yes, to avoid injury—but most out of simple pride in his own beautiful skill; he sent home a javelin.

The stallion buried deep and powerfully that barb, his thick body shuddering, groaning; the mare both fought and welcomed that which she most desired, the huge and penetrating rage of the stallion's passion to possess.

'Do your stuff, old peckerhead,' was all Hazard said. 'I think we've got an audience.'

14

The prepotency of a Lepage stud is such that three of five colts are born blue roan. Of those three, two will have a star on the forehead; but the third will be the total blue of the original mustang. Poseidon did not have the star; nor did the four stallions between him and the nameless original.

The first time Hazard saw the mustang colt that was to be founder of the line—the first time he saw *them*, I should say, for there were two of them, the mustang and the Cree—they were together out in the middle of Wildfire Lake.

It was as if they had just bobbed to the surface. Hazard had looked a minute earlier and there was nothing to be seen but whitecaps; he was up on a high bank that is almost a cliff; he was there partly just to look, partly because he was homesick for the sight of a little water. The flat parklands break suddenly, and you see a valley—not in front of you. Below you. The squares of farm-land are gone and below you a wooded coulee, like the crack in a fat lady's arse, guides a scar of earth down to a long narrow lake. The man in the water wasn't riding the horse; he was swimming beside it with his arm around its neck, as if one or the other of them was about to drown.

Hazard raced down that high hill so recklessly he might have broken every bone in his body; he stripped off his green plaid mackinaw—it was a raw windy day in late fall. He was a har-vester then, come west for the first time, and he was unbearably homesick. He kicked off his boots and started into that cold lake; but just as he did so the swimmer, who as I say turned out to be a Cree—at least I discovered years later there were some Crees at the outlet of the lake that fall, drying fish—he got into the shallows and managed to stand up. He was pulling not a horse but a very young colt, his arm around its neck. The colt was so exhausted it had quit trying, and the Indian was pulling it through the water.

Just as Hazard got his crotch wet, however, the Indian stepped into a hole. Then Hazard too hit deep water and had to strike out swimming; but Hazard practically grew up in the water. The Indian came to the surface and went down again; indeed, he had gone down for the third time, still clinging to the colt, when Hazard dived, and in the green haze of that pure water caught hold of the man's black hair and hauled him up head first.

A strange thing happened. Hazard should have told the man to let go of the colt so they'd stand a decent chance of getting to shore. Instead he pitched in like a madman, thrashing and struggling to save both.

When they got up onto a sandbar, the Cree knelt to massage the colt's heart, gasping for breath himself, unable to get to his own feet. Hazard began to feel very much the intruder; he walked ashore and busied himself putting on his boots—only to turn on an impulse and walk boots and all back into the water; he carried the Indian, then the colt, out onto the beach. It was a male colt, a stallion. Hazard studied first the colt, then the Indian, and noticed the latter had in his long hair a couple of very fat lice; they too had narrowly escaped drowning. I saved them too, he thought to himself, and chuckled even while he panted. He shivered from the raw wind on his wet clothes; he stood shivering, chuckling, panting like an utter idiot, yet he was unable to tear himself away.

The colt opened his big gentle eyes and the Cree turned to Hazard for the first time, grinning now. Hazard was startled, for the Indian had the physique of a young man; yet his few remaining teeth looked nothing less than ancient.

'I saved your colt,' the Indian said.

'It isn't mine.'

The Indian smiled his disbelief. 'Don't fear. I shall demand nothing.'

Hazard started to answer, but instead he picked up his mackinaw and knelt and began rubbing fiercely at the colt's pale blue, silky coat. He paused to wring the icy water from his beard, then would not waste time on anything so trivial.

Now, while Hazard laboured, the Indian stood watching. 'I demand nothing,' he repeated.

He was wearing only moccasins and a pair of badly soiled tweed dress trousers. He pulled something that looked like an eagle feather from his pocket and stuck it into one of his braids. Then—and Hazard swore to this—he brought out a small pocket mirror and looked at himself. 'I saved your colt,' he said.

'It is not mine,' Hazard tried to explain. 'I'm a stranger here myself.'

The Indian's old teeth were beginning to chatter; he must have been in the water a long time. He said something like, '*Kis-see-wus-kut-tā-o.*'

'Stranger,' Hazard said. He guessed that perhaps the Indian spoke little English. 'Me stranger. Me no live here.'

The Indian shook his head. His teeth were chattering uncontrollably. 'I do not wish to be thanked. It is enough to have saved your colt. *Kis-see-wus-kut-tā-o.*'

'Wait a minute,' Hazard said. 'Hang on.' The Cree gave the impression that he was about to leave. 'You can't just take off. You can't just march away from this motherless colt. My God, it'll die of starvation. You can't just stick a feather into your bonnet and go high-tailing off into the weeds. We'll have to find out who owns—'

But indeed the Indian had gone. They were up on the sandy beach in a small opening beside a heavy stand of spruce and balm of Gilead and a lot of underbrush—or rather, Hazard was: the Cree was gone into the grove. 'Hang on!' Hazard yelled. 'Wait! Stop!' He hesitated, looking at the colt, looking at the point where a sapling quivered. Then it struck him; that mysterious bird might be a horse thief. Hazard went into underbrush, hollering and flailing. He slashed his eyes and they watered and he had to stand still; and then, all of a sudden, rubbing away the tears, he saw he had stepped into a clearing.

It was a tiny clearing, just large enough for a grave. At the foot of a tall tamarack was a rectangle of water-worn stones and set at one end, on the far side from the tamarack, was a small unpainted wooden cross. On the cross was a five-pound syrup pail (Hazard opened it) containing a handful of wooden matches, a packet of tea leaves, a white paper bag full of sugar. Without thinking, Hazard went back to the colt. He wrapped his mackinaw over its shoulders and picked it up; and only then, standing firm and stocky with the colt in his arms, did he wonder what he was going to do.

He asked himself a question, not recognizing that the answer would be twenty-four years of wandering, of leading a stallion from farm to farm. He stood alone, puzzled, homesick; and all he could think of was a building he had vaguely glimpsed as he charged down the hill. Now he looked up: and he saw on the hill's crest a large and solitary house.

I have climbed that hill with nothing to burden me but a pailful of saskatoons. Halfway up I had no choice but to fasten the pail by its handle to my belt and seize at clumps of grass with my bare hands, meanwhile driving my toes into the crumbling clay. Hazard, more on his knees than on his feet, somehow carried a colt to the top.

The mansion was deserted. Hazard took the liberty of walking in. He found a long couch in the library and he put down the colt. He found in the kitchen a stove, a box of blue-headed matches, and piled in the centre of the floor what must have been a cord of firewood. Hazard could not know that the owner was three years dead, his will a tangle that to this day goes unriddled.

He ignored the film of dust on the chrome-frilled and tile-decorated cookstove; he lifted the cast iron lids and shaved a stick of dry wood onto a handful of crumpled pages from a book on horse breeding. He struck a match on the stove poker and lit the paper and began to adjust the dampers.

He went for milk and medicine, he went to collect the wages he had coming from the boss of a threshing crew: and he not only saved but raised the colt.

15

Hazard never gave a name to that first stallion, since he believed it already to have a name when it became his; nor did he ever yield to the obvious temptation to call it, simply, Lepage. Yet in later years he could not help but speculate, ruminating about the past, and at various times he toyed with Morning Sun (although he found the colt in late afternoon), Woodpecker, Spud Island, Hind and Cuneiform. On one occasion I timidly suggested the name Charles Lamb, explaining my intent in choosing that name; Hazard rejected my suggestion outright and, I thought, somewhat hastily. At any rate, the generations appeared: Compass by—let us say, Hind—out of a one-eyed mare that lived for eight years in a coalmine; Scupper got by Compass out of Dumpling, an excellent cowpony owned by a rustler in the Cree River hills—in each of these cases Hazard had to buy back the perfect get at a cost vastly exceeding the charge for the original service; Bluenose got by Scupper out of Old May, a schoolhorse belonging to a family of Mennonites who were leaving for Mexico; Tiller got by Bluenose out of Queenie, the best drayhorse in the town of Burkhardt; Poseidon, got by Tiller out of a nameless white horse that was abandoned in Notikeewin by a travelling circus.

Hazard had a certain flourish with names. In the reign of Compass, especially, he came very near to flourishing himself. He had of his own in the valley along the lake a herd of forty horses, as well as a waiting list of farmers' mares. He travelled two purebred stallions in addition to his own excellent breed: a Clydesdale and a quarter horse. By 1928 he was planning to build barns around the isolated mansion in which he lived. One year later he could hardly afford the feed to see his herd through the terrible winter of '29. By 1932, when he became engaged, he had secretly to sell a team of Lepage geldings in order to buy Martha a ring.

I wish I could report that the breeding of an unknown filly in a deserted summer resort restored Hazard's dream to its original flush and vigour. But even as he carefully wiped down the parts of his silent stallion, Hazard had a suspicion the jump did not catch. And he was further made uneasy by the pair of dark eyes that watched for a considerable while from under a nearby spruce, only to disappear when Hazard went to find a damp cloth.

The patient Indian, in his enthusiasm at the spectacle, hurried immediately to a filling station where he complimented the mare's owner on his choice of stallion. The startled owner, who had no desire to breed his mares, thereupon called up the town constable from his afternoon couch; the constable in turn put on his badge of authority and went to the local bootlegger and notified the magistrate, who was just then quenching his afternoon's thirst, that he could by the simple expedient of a conviction earn his customary two-dollar fee.

Hazard, had he not delayed, hoping in four hours to permit Poseidon again to stand for service, might by this time have been far distant from town. Instead he was gathering sticks and twigs and building a fire beside a sign that read:

HORSES
STRICTLY PROHIBITED
ON BEACH

And he was squatting down to eat from a can of beans when the constable summoned him.

The combination firehall-jail-magistrate's office-bingo palace was a considerable distance inland from shore. The magistrate, a certain Mr Flood, was a retired railroader whose concept of justice had a great deal to do with punctuality.

Hazard was late: he was offered somewhat abruptly a chair beside a very warm oil heater, so situated that he faced not the magistrate's desk but rather a bookshelf.

'Well, Reverend,' the magistrate began. 'Good to see you at last. And have you the papers with you?'

'The papers, sir?'

'The documents, Reverend.'

Hazard had the distinct impression he was being questioned by a row of leather-bound books. The heat from the heater came up over him like a wave. 'The papers,' he pronounced again, with growing difficulty.

'Tut, tut, Reverend. We must have the papers. The usual identification, you know.' The magistrate, because Hazard was late, had found time to consult a number of the volumes with which he had been provided by a generous government. He put a finger to the volume open on the desk and read slowly: 'An Act for the Enrolment of Stallions'. To Hazard he said, 'The beast in question must be registered if order is to prevail. We must see the papers.' To the constable he said, 'Bring in Mr Running Post.'

The Indian, a quiet-spoken and shy fellow somewhat advanced in years, was promptly called in from outside the open door. He slipped something into the left pocket of his denim shirt as he entered the room; then he attempted to keep the Bible that was offered him. Standing at rigid attention, he gave so fine and accurate an account of what had transpired on the lot of a cabin bearing the name Weehafun that Hazard spontaneously nodded his head.

The magistrate was equally delighted. But soon he encountered difficulty in locating the passage which bore relevance to Hazard's obvious guilt. Embarrassed, finally, by his own confusion, he put a middle finger to a passage seemingly at random and read in a loud and very authoritative voice: 'In particular, every inspector shall report any and every grave defect of conformation in any such stallion, and (if such there be) any bone-spavin, bog-spavin, ring-bone, side-bone, or curb, apparently due to defective conformation or structural weakness, and any cataract, amaurosis, periodic ophthalmia (moon-blindness), laryngeal hemiplegia (roaring or whistling), chorea (spring-halt) or St Vitus' Dance, or any condition rendering it, in the judgment of the inspector, unfit for breeding purposes.'

Hazard, slowly, rose up from his chair to his feet: 'A healthier horse than mine has never walked, run or stood for service.' He sat down.

'Is this then true?' the magistrate inquired sternly.

Both the Indian and the constable concurred, the constable going so far as to compliment Poseidon on the way he was hung, though in fact it was the Indian who had witnessed the consummation: thus truth passes into legend.

'Excellent,' the magistrate said. 'Excellent. Then, while we must convict, we are able to convict with compassion and leniency.' He pointed again at his book: 'Section 18: Penalty . . . Hmmm . . .' He looked directly across the room at the constable. 'That will be twenty dollars cash.'

72

Hazard was staring at the bookshelf; he was content to let his eyelids slide slowly down over his eyes, the books blurring . . .

The constable spoke: 'The owner shall pay to any person capturing or impounding an entire animal, for each stallion, bull or jackass, three dollars, for each boar, ram or he-goat, two dollars. . . .'

Hazard knew he must protest.

But the Indian was speaking: 'As poundkeeper I must charge a fee of fifty cents per day for the care and sustenance of a stallion, and for a gelding—'

Mr Flood rapped his desk with a gavel.

'I haven't got it,' Hazard explained sleepily, trying to sit up straight in his chair beside the heater. He emptied the contents of all his pockets into the constable's hands: and yet he was able to produce from his borrowed black suit only one Irish Sweepstake ticket, one rubber glove, and enough cash to satisfy the magistrate, the poundkeeper, and the nameless constable. HIS MAJESTY, by and with the advice and consent of the Legislative Assembly of Alberta, had twenty dollars coming.

Mr Flood put a finger to the text before him. 'Then, my good Reverend, I must sentence you to a term of imprisonment not exceeding one month.' He motioned the constable to join him behind the desk. The two men whispered together. 'However,' the magistrate went on to Hazard, smiling to himself, then at the constable, 'in view of your calling we have resolved to make allowances. We take it you are a compassionate man?'

Hazard started to ask a question but only nodded instead.

'You are an all-round sort of fellow, it would appear?' the magistrate continued.

Hazard raised a hand to protest; the gesture was transformed by his silence into a blessing.

'We have on the outskirts of our fair little village,' Mr Flood concluded, 'a woman who most urgently requires some physical assistance. While your horses must stay in the pound, you have the generous choice of spending nine days in jail, or three days on the farm earning an honest dollar, helping the poor indigent widow. Choose now.'

D

But before he could stir himself awake and answer, the three waiting men burst into loud laughter.

16

Snow was beginning to fall next morning as the constable, a quiet, rather formal, yet sympathetic man after all, drove Hazard out to what proved to be a stump ranch; a clearing in the bush that pretended feebly at being a grain farm. Hazard had slept but fitfully on the planks in a tiny and draughty cell: he abhorred cramped spaces. The windshield wipers on the constable's little car were not working and poor uneasy Hazard, after what was in fact quite a long drive, stepped suddenly from behind the thick white window before his eyes into the manure in front of Mrs Lank's log barn.

The manure pile, because it generated its own heat within, had not frozen; Hazard sank to his ankles and was at the same time blinded by the white glare of the falling snow. As he swung his arms to keep his balance, labouring to free his feet, he heard a voice of indeterminate sex cry out, 'And Adam . . . begat a son in his own likeness, after his own image . . .'

Hazard turned to see a woman with slacks under her skirt pumping wildly at a short pump handle. She did this with one hand; with the other she held a pail to a spout from which came only a trickle of water: as she worked so violently her breasts bobbed up and down like cats put to drown in a sack.

The local pig-sticker had already performed his function; a carcass was hung by its hind legs from a singletree in the doorway of the log barn. The sticker, after killing, bleeding and scalding the pig, had scraped off its bristles, then had cut the cord out of the skin at the back of both hind legs below the knee. He had hooked in the singletree, which in turn was fastened to a wire stretcher. The carcass now hung head downward, but the head

74

was already cut off just behind the ears and lying on its flat side, bleeding brightly into the fresh snow.

The moment Hazard was free of the manure, the sticker, a rather young man, gaunt and shy, gathered together his knives; he picked up the pig's head by one ear, climbed into the seat that Hazard had vacated. The car went racing and skidding away down the lane.

Hazard had many times and generously helped his neighbours butcher, receiving in return a few pounds of fresh meat. Now he was quick to make himself useful, remembering the constable on the drive out had jokingly mentioned the need to murder only a couple of hogs. One was halfway to the pork barrel. In his ignorance Hazard saw no reason why he might not finish his task and be back to Poseidon by nightfall.

Quickly he cut out the penis and slit the skin of the belly back almost to the anus; he was tying a knot in the urethra when Mrs Lank brought him his first cup of coffee.

It was a welcome hot drink, and the coffee cake that went with it was absolutely delicious. Next Hazard took hold of the pig's tail and held it firmly in his left hand while he cut a circle around the anus, careful not to slice into the colon. Carefully he brought the colon forward and held it shut with his hand while Mrs Lank modestly tied a piece of twine around it. During this operation Hazad first noticed that the lady, though in the habit of chewing snuff, had vivacious blue eyes.

'That'll do it,' Hazard said, finishing the knot himself. 'Now if you'll run get me something to catch the guts in when I slit the belly all the way down. And I'll need a saw for those ribs.'

Mrs Lank went into the barn and picked up a galvanized washtub she'd set on the steps leading up to the little loft above her two cows. With a rather dull butcher knife Hazard sliced a neat line through the skin and fat between the two rows of six nipples, careful not to cut into the small intestine. Already he was cursing the sticker for what seemed a hasty and unnecessary departure. 'Will you want me to clean these intestines for sausage ?'

'We can do it together,' she said. 'Would you like more coffee ?'

Hazard said he would, and the widow disappeared into the swirling gentle snowfall towards her shack. Now Hazard, casting about, found an old handsaw on the stoneboat on which the pig had been scraped. A barrel of water stood nearby, the hot water steaming into the chill air. Hazard rinsed the saw and squatted down to see where he must cut through the ribs.

He had some difficulty, and just as he was about to finish, Mrs Lank came up behind him with more coffee and some freshly baked macaroons. 'Here you go—you said your name was—'

'Hazard.'

'Try these, Reverend Hazard.'

Macaroons (and this was uncanny) were his favourite cookies. He straightened up, the saw in his hand, warm grease on its teeth; before he could speak there came the sound of fat ripping, and the guts tumbled into the galvanized tub. Hazard put the saw down on the stoneboat and turned into Mrs Lank's smiling face.

The tub of guts smoked into the chill air. In a short while there would come warm days and muddy roads and the first buzz of flies; this was perfect butchering weather. Hazard began to feel pride in his work; he felt even a touch of warmth towards the woman who was now dipping into an open red box of Copenhagen snuff. The guts almost filled the battered old washtub. The full white bladder was the size of a baseball. The stomach was white, the large intestine smooth and a misty blue, the small intestine wrinkled and pink.

Hazard, relaxed and feeling almost jovial, handed the empty cup to the widow and picked up his knife; he was making good time. He bent and cut free the liver; he cut off the bright blue gall and dropped the liver into a pail of cold water.

Two cats that had come down from the barn loft now sniffed and pawed at a kidney Hazard threw to them on the snow.

'Could you eat heart for dinner, Reverend Hazard?'

He fished through the tub with his bare hands and the knife for a place to cut. The lungs and heart came up together; the lungs, full of blood, were bright red, like a giant rose. Hazard sliced the heart free; with his thumb he flicked a dark clot of blood out of each of the four chambers, onto the red snow.

Romance will somehow find a way into our lives. Surely Hazard and I were alike in strenuously resisting that distortion of facts by which men delude themselves. Mine is a conservative temperament. Hazard was perhaps less disciplined than I; as a result his sympathies, if not always his passions, were wont to corrupt his joy in simple things.

By 11.35 in the morning, he had pretty much finished with the first pig. He went to the kitchen door and called to Mrs Lank: 'Where's that other hog?'

Mrs Lank told him; Hazard went back to the barn and sharpened the old butcher knife on a worn carborundum stone. He went to the rear stall, where the two pigs had been fattened together. He crawled into the stall where a sow moved its snout nervously about in an empty trough. Hazard, looking at the sharpened blade, then at the sow's neck, hesitated; as he did so Mrs Lank appeared with a large basin.

'This will do to catch the blood,' Mrs Lank said.

'The blood?' Hazard said.

'For the blood sausage,' Mrs Lank explained, handing him the basin. 'The trick is,' she added with a smile, 'to avoid the heart. So the pig will bleed properly.'

Hazard felt he must use both hands to support the weight of the knife. 'Isn't it about dinnertime?' he wondered. 'Right after we eat . . .'

The linen tablecloth was covered with silver, with china and candles; Hazard feared he might swoon with hunger. His crystal wine glass was filled and refilled with rhubarb wine. The widow had heard of his crime; but she, unlike his prosecutors, was all sympathy. She asked that Hazard describe in detail his gorgeous stud and wished with a sigh that he might have his just desserts. Her hands bumped Hazard's over the empty plates and their full glasses of wine; he seemed to be without touch. An old perfume emanated from between her breasts (and she had put on her Sunday dress); he could not smell. They talked. They nodded and laughed and drank. Poor dear ignorant Hazard, his soulful dark eyes lost in concern for his impounded horses, was ready to devour the very knives and forks themselves.

What Hazard finally ate he never told me; he was quite too dizzy to know. That the sticker failed to show up in the afternoon, he did remember. And he recalled preparing a crock of brine in the small cellar under the shack, adding salt to the water in the crock until an egg floated.

Supper proved to be another large helping of silver, china, linen, candlelight and rhubarb wine. It was only after the meal had been served and eaten that Hazard realized he was in genuine trouble.

The shack contained only one bedroom.

A sofa in the living room could, if necessary, be turned into a makeshift and very uncomfortable bed. Mrs Lank failed to offer him any blankets, and when he sat down on the sofa and pulled off his shoes, she sat down beside him.

But Hazard was loyal to his own resolve that night. He pretended to stomach cramps, and the wine of noon and evening had made this something of a fact. Mrs Lank offered him more coffee, obviously intending to keep him awake forever. He insisted the coffee was giving him a headache—and he lay curled up and jittery under his black suitcoat on the sofa for seven hours; in the morning his back was so sore the pain was scarcely to be endured.

By ten o'clock that morning the pig-sticker still had not returned. Now the widow invited Hazard to get on with the killing; this time she herself sharpened another knife, more like a bayonet, on the carborundum stone, and she led Hazard to the back stall.

And then it came in full force to Hazard's mind: the knife entering the throat, his hand becoming sticky as the blood ran wet and warm down the knife's handle; the hollow rasp of the pig's breathing as it stood braced on its four legs; the front knees beginning to tremble; the blood gurgling from the small slit in the throat; the steady bright gush dwindling to a trickle. The pig.

The horse. The horse. The pig. In all the violent yokings of Greek wisdom, in all its peculiar combinations of the parts of different animals, of the parts of animals and men, I have found no reference to a creature half horse, half hog.

And now Hazard thought of the sow going down on its front knees, silent, its eyes open but looking at nothing. He thought of the pig collapsing on to its side and beginning to thresh, still silent, at each kick the blood spurting bright—

Dear reader, I ask you, forgive, forgive the erring man. But he could not bring himself to kill; he could not bring himself to do it. And what alternative did he have? How could he, honourably, refuse to perform the appointed task?

The widow threw some chop to to the sow.

17

Hazard was shortly to hanker for the quiet of the little cell from which he had so happily fled only the previous morning. To put the problem, in all kindness, baldly—Mrs Lank, the widow in question, had an uncontrollable urge to have the one thing of which she said she had been deprived by life: that is, the pleasure of being got with child. She was desperate to distraction, unbeknownst to Hazard, to perpetuate herself and the memory of her dear dead husband in the usual preposterous fashion.

To the male reader this assignment might indeed sound like a veritable return to the Garden of Eden. I remarked as much to Hazard when first he mentioned the incident.

He groaned. He clutched at his private parts. Then he burst out, or wailed rather, 'Kee-rist all smothering fishhooks.' Then he began to rock as if in great pain.

Hazard himself claimed—and he was not a man given to maligning others—she was the ugliest woman he ever laid eyes on. Twice while I was talking he fell asleep in the afternoon, only to begin threshing and gagging. 'What's the matter?' I asked, shaking him to wake him up. He sometimes dozed off in the hot sun while I was asking questions and making notes. 'That woman was ugly,' he said on both occasions, and went back to sleep.

'Then why did you do it?' I tried to ask him.

As they threshed and bucked in the musty hay in the hayloft, Hazard and Mrs Lank, he too asked himself, 'How did I get here? Is this then justice? Would it not have been simpler to stick the sow?' As they bucked and threshed, the hay proving so dusty that both on occasion sneezed, the widow cried out, 'O that it might be a son.' And as she cried out, her strong hands clutching Hazard's bare buttocks (his pants were tangled around his knees), he was filled with a purpose that transcended despair.

Hazard, against his own will, became obsessed with the notion that she must be got pregnant.

Understand, he had hardly two days left at his disposal. But worse—he had somehow to summon up his lust so he might be able to approach that really peculiar-looking woman. And he could hardly, after all, go time and time again as if to stab the poor innocent pig, thus driving himself into the refuge of Mrs Lank's waiting arms.

No, Hazard, whose imagination had stopped him from killing the fat sow, found also a means to stimulate his faltering need. The imagination plays strange tricks. One hour later Hazard and the lusting old sack of a woman were again knocking together, now in the bed he had avoided all night, and while Mrs Lank imagined the child she was certain she would have, Hazard imagined—may heaven forgive him—the woman to whom he was engaged.

Hazard, of course, was under the impression that Martha, a virgin, was capable of loving none other than he. And he imagined himself at last plucking the fruit of his long season. He was, in his mind's eye, driving the very horn of his impatience into the hot and yielding flesh.

'What's the matter?' Mrs Lank whispered at dawn.

'My eyes,' Hazard said. 'Even my eyes are tired.'

But he slugged away at his terrible task.

'Ah, Reverend,' the widow giggled. 'Don't hurt your back.'

He kissed her bruised lips into a necessary silence. In his mind's ear he heard Martha assuring him: 'Not *again*, Hazard, you rascal.' And in his head he saw her body beneath his own, her great soft breasts like pillows to his sorrow, her thighs warm and urgent even to his failing member, her belly damp with their mingled joy and sweat.

They were two long days. The widow bathed Hazard's sore body if not her own, massaged his failing back, anointed him here and there with goose grease, carried rhubarb wine to where he lay spent—and always dreaming—amidst the unwashed bed-clothes, sometimes on the bed, sometimes on the dusty floor.

When a knock came at the door of the shack, Hazard went to answer. Had it been the pig-sticker he would have offered his own throat. The constable stood in the doorway, grinning from ear to ear. 'Are you finished?' he asked.

Hazard, when he told me the story, buried his head in his arms. 'I can't imagine—' I began to interrupt at one point. 'Two days and two nights,' he said, his groan changing to a kind of helpless laugh; one got the impression that all time and all leisure could not erase the stain from his hurt mind. 'And yet I was a driven man. There was no let-up. She lent a helping hand and I did my best.'

18

I have never been able to trace Mrs Lank; but surely it would not be wrong to suppose her disappearance was the consequence of Hazard's success. I choose to think so, and I make no apologies. It may be that she returned to New Brunswick; the postmaster was given an address there, but no mail ever came to be for-warded. Her husband was from that distant part of the world; he perished at sea when he volunteered for a dangerous naval mission. Hazard, after reclaiming Poseidon and his rig, drove away stone broke from the pound and the tattle-tale Indian. I did for a few minutes one night get hold of that Mr Running Post, but he had been drinking. He recalled vaguely a very attractive widow who owned a farm that fronted on the lake: she made a good deal of money after the war when the boom in summer cottages began. This widow of the Indian's memory, however, stood well over six feet: Hazard mentioned no such bulk or size.

The difficulties of the encounter with Mrs Lank had purged Hazard of at least some of his silliness; without the slightest hesitation he set about pursuing his ultimate goal. Five miles out of town he came to a farm that had on it a red horse barn that was obviously in use. He turned in at the lane.

The horrors of the recent past were shortly to be compounded by those of the immediate future. He was cursed by a hired man whom he awakened from a daytime nap. Undeterred, he turned in at a second long lane, then into a field where a man was using a team to pull a manure spreader, then into a yard that was full of machinery for haying.

Time and again he knew insult. He endured the false accusations of a woman who did not want her children to know that animals like Poseidon existed. He was chased from a barbed wire gate by two yapping dogs that were sicked on the heels of his horses. He was, he believed, one time shot at from an attic window. But he was not asked to breed so much as a solitary mare.

Hazard was turned and mocked away from where he would once have been more than welcome. He was not offered a stall for the night for his stallion; he was not offered either food or drink for himself. Fortunately God in His infinite mercy has strewn the roads of Alberta with empty beer bottles that might be picked up and sold at twenty cents a dozen. This manna, revealed in abundance by the melting of the snow, was sufficient to keep Hazard alive.

If you look at a map of Alberta you will recognize that, travelling from Mrs Lank's stump ranch eastward into the parklands, Hazard must inevitably have driven along the road that is visible from my bathroom window.

By a fortunate combination of light and reflection, I am able to see out of my window without leaving my bathtub. A mirror is so placed above my sink that I have been able to sit for hours, attempting to imagine what in fact did happen (allowing for the reversal of the image) exactly where I imagine it. It is then *time* that I must reconstruct, not space. Further, I am able to see far distant; it is what is nearest that I cannot always make out from my high window. Nearest and just below me, across an impeccable lawn, a wall of spruce trees screens what is a children's playground. While adults are encouraged to visit on these brick and stucco premises, children are encouraged to wait outside, playing. The arched entryway into the playground, which should afford me a glimpse through the trees, is obscured by a totem pole. The gift of an anonymous donor, approximately twenty feet in height, the pole has on its top a grotesque bird with outstretched wings; beneath the bird (an eagle?) are three distorted faces which are nevertheless human. Over the top of the bird's head and beak (it is surely not a raven) I am able easily to see a road and beside it a field in which, each spring, a lone farmer sweats and labours to break up a few more acres of virgin land.

Hazard, with his two horses and his milk-wagon, passed along that same distant road at 9.45 on the morning of Wednesday, 28 March, and had I been here then I might have seen him as he moseyed along, enjoying the spring day; I might even have glimpsed the unlikely passenger he had picked up in a small beer parlour the day before. But I was, as you may recall, in Coulee Hill.

I have met and talked with, albeit only for half an hour, this fellow Eugene Utter; he was a windbag from beginning to end. He had with him, both when I saw him and when he met Hazard, nothing but a large black leather suitcase.

Hazard felt much dejected at the frustration his visit to various farms had caused him; in his dejection he resorted to the occational glass of beer. I seldom touch alcohol, recognizing as I do that it only blurs one's precision of thought and feeling. Hazard drank: his little spell of the blues became worse.

He was moping over a fourth glass when the stranger accosted him, arguing without provocation that Hazard should employ not one horse but a team to pull the milk-wagon parked beside the men's outhouse behind the little brick hotel.

'And just where in hell,' Hazard replied, 'would I find *another* horse?'

'That's what I'm here for,' the stranger replied.

'Have a beer,' Hazard replied.

'Ah yes. Much obliged.' The stranger sat down, offering a big hand at the same time. 'Utter is the name. Eugene. Dealer in everything and anything.' He held in his left hand his suitcase. 'I know a friend in need when I see one.'

Hazard, in shaking the man's hand, noticed two fingers were missing. 'I am not a man of the cloth,' he said, defensively tugging at the beard that hid his collar.

Utter helped himself to the half of Hazard's beer that remained on the table and signalled for another round even before the first had been delivered. 'That old gelding out there belongs to a man who doesn't know horseflesh from mink feed.'

'Mink feed your ass,' Hazard replied. 'That old gelding enables me to lead a fresh young stallion from farm to farm to farm throughout the entire length and breadth of this province, and into Saskatchewan if necessary.'

It was one of the peculiarities of this Utter fellow that he inspired others to excess. 'And to what end,' he asked politely of Hazard, 'may I ever so humbly inquire, do you go on leading—'

'To the end that any time that same stud screws anything that stands on four legs I pocket three bucks cash.'

The waiter just then brought two rounds and Utter announced that he was broke. Hazard paid, remarking as he did so: 'Mares are scarce.'

'In some little hick town east of here,' Utter countered, 'I saw five beautiful mares in one corral. Or I believe it was a skating rink.'

Hazard hesitated, a glass of beer halfway to his lips. 'Coulee Hill?' he inquired.

'Ah yes,' Utter said. 'Coulee Hill. A pleasant enough dump. I had a few beers in the Coulee Hill Hotel—' he scratched at the old blue shirt that covered his belly—'it must have been less than a week ago.'

As I have already admitted, I did speak briefly one afternoon to a man who answered to Utter's description: fierce blue eyes, blond hair that might have been combed a month earlier, two fingers missing from his right hand, a full blond beard. We had a short but vehement argument about the Stanley Cup play-offs; I happen to be an expert on hockey. But this Utter, self-proclaimed champion of something or other, gave to Hazard a tidbit of gossip which I can only reject as fallacious if not malicious.

'She lives right there in the hotel?' Utter said when Hazard commented on Martha's living in Coulee Hill. 'Ah yes.' He was fond of saying, especially of his own remarks, ah yes. 'That tall woman—a mane of hair like a fountain of honey.'

'My purpose in life,' Hazard said.

'Well then,' Utter said, ordering with a generous flourish of his three-fingered hand another beer, 'you better close the barn door before it's too late. There's a lanky moon-faced kid mooning after her night and day. A look in his eye like a pig pissing.'

'You must be thinking of the wrong town,' Hazard said. 'We've been engaged—' he made a mental calculation—'it will be thirteen or fourteen years this spring.'

'A lovely pair of tits, this woman,' Utter said. 'Large.'

'And firm,' Hazard said. 'My dear God, you could chip your teeth.'

'Ah yes,' Utter said. 'Then hustle home. Or moonface won't have a tooth in his mouth.'

'He won't have a tooth in his mouth after I get there,' Hazard ventured.

'If you looked at him hard,' Utter said, 'I believe he'd fall flat on his ass. Gawky sort of kid. Hardly throws a shadow. All head—big brooding eyes set too close together, a hatchet nose and his hair down over—'

'I'll boot his ass up between his eyebrows,' Hazard said. He picked up a glass of tomato juice to make red eye out of his fresh glass of beer.

But his show of nonchalance was just that. 'Drink up,' he said twice in the next ten minutes.

Hazard knew his arbitrary and high-handed rule was being challenged, his era might draw to a close. Inside of an hour he and Eugene Utter were heading east, Utter on the lookout for more empty bottles, jumping off the wagon now and then to pick one out of the dry grass or the crocuses or the pussy willows while the gelding walked on; Hazard brooding, uneasy, and always hurrying his horses forward—on the pretext of believing his passenger would soon locate a mare.

19

By dint of working past sundown, Utter came up with twenty-four dozen empties; enough to set the milk-wagon to jingling. The obvious place to sell empty beer bottles is in a small-town beer parlour; one thing led to another. Hazard, who ordinarily drank moderately, drank to excess. Under the stimulation of his merry shouts and vigorous commands, beer flowed. He remembered only vaguely entering into the men's toilet and finding Utter leaning forward over the second of two urinals, his left hand against the wall above the urinal, his right invisible between the white enamel wings of the urinal itself.

Hazard stood up to the first urinal.

Utter now whispered without looking up: 'There's a fellow at our table who claims he owns one hell of a fine mare. I'm going to do a little dickering if it's all right with you.'

'By all means,' Hazard said. 'Do whatever you think best.'

'I've got him in a bind,' Utter said. 'He's a dumb farmer. Wants to get to a big wedding somewhere across the river.'

'A wedding?' Hazard inquired, leaning closer into the urinal.

'I've got him by the short hairs,' Utter insisted. 'How can he

86

travel sixty miles with a two-horse wagon and one horse? He needs the price of a train ticket.'

'I think I just spent our last cent on that last round,' Hazard said.

A third man now entered the toilet.

'First,' Utter said, 'we'll trade off the milk-wagon—'

'That milk-wagon yours?' the new arrival said. 'It'd make a damned fine school outfit.'

Now two more men pushed their way into the small toilet. Utter backed away from his urinal, caught with a thumb and forefinger his clothes, eased himself back inside his underwear, and went towards the sink. But the second of the two newest arrivals had already stepped up to the sink and opened his fly. Utter turned back to the man who had replaced him at the second urinal. 'What would you offer me?'

'Ten dollars spot cash—'

'Throw in the horse,' the man at the sink said, 'and I'll make it fifteen.'

Now it was Hazard's turn to turn away from the first urinal. He could not get back to the door, for another fellow, the farmer who owned the mare, was trying to crowd his way in. There was to the right of both urinals (the sink was on the left) an old bathtub: Hazard stepped into the bathtub and sat down.

'Is that horse for sale?' the farmer at the door said. 'I'll give you twenty bucks on the barrelhead, and you can keep the milk-wagon. I'm on my way to a wedding—'

'Anybody we know?' the man at the first urinal asked.

'One of Tad Proudfoot's boys,' the farmer said. 'The old bastard still owes me twenty bucks for a load of bones—'

Hazard was sleepy. Twenty dollars sounded like a good enough price.

'What do you say to that?' Utter said.

'We need a mare,' Hazard said.

'Leave it to me,' Utter said. 'Here, hold this for a minute.' He handed two ten-dollar bills to Hazard and turned once again to the farmer who was now putting away his wallet with his right hand while using his left to guide a bright stream of urine into a distant urinal.

'Where'd you lose two fingers?' the man at the first urinal asked.

'Fighting for liberty,' Utter said.

The man who had urinated in the sink now turned on a tap in the bathtub in order to wash his hands. Hazard, surprised by the water in his shoes, looked up and saw his own face at the tub's edge in the mirror that was leaned against the wall under the sink.

'Hey,' the man who was washing his hands said, noticing that Hazard held two ten-dollar bills. 'Why don't we get a case of *Lethbridge* to take out? They're flicking the lights now to close the bar.'

20

By an irony which I propose to explain later, I had received a copy of the same invitation as that which the anonymous farmer carried in his pocket:

Mr and Mrs Nicholas Melnyk
request the honour of your presence
at the marriage of their daughter
Catherine
to
Mr Tiberius Torbay Proudfoot
on Monday, the second of April
nineteen hundred and forty-five
at eleven o'clock
St Vladimir's Ukrainian Orthodox Church
New Galway, Alberta

I need not describe the card itself, with its cross of silver, its green sprig (was it of olive?), and its embossed inscription: HOLY SACRAMENT OF MATRIMONY.

Hazard, in the company of the man whom he had mistaken for a friend, set out on a frantic search for the stallion which they had in error sold for twenty dollars. The farmer had disappeared with the blue horse and his own fine mare. The money itself had been spent on beer and a comfortable hotel room.

The questing pair came on Easter Sunday—Easter was on 1 April that year—to the Cree River: only to discover the river was so in flood the bridge had gone out.

Hazard had some acquaintance with that region. Morosely he explained to Utter that the nearest bridge was fourteen miles away in the wrong direction; farther than they could possibly travel in time to get to the wedding the next day.

Utter raised his right hand, from which the index and middle fingers were missing. 'It was my good fortune in my youth to act as did nature herself; I too destroyed a bridge.'

'And damned near got killed,' Hazard said.

'Ah yes. I was fool enough to rely on a human mechanism, in that case, a pocket watch, to time my creation. I hardly deserved to escape alive.'

'Let's go back to the nearest beer—' And then Hazard remembered it was Sunday.

'I am only sorry for your sake,' Utter said. 'Liquor will flow extravagantly at this wedding. Heaps and platters of food will make the tables groan at the dead weight of gluttony. Unmarried young ladies will have gathered from miles about: the sinful dancing will go on for two days. Because of the muddy spring roads, many guests will be compelled to travel by horse.'

Satan could not have offered a temptation of more grotesque subtlety.

'Can you swim?' Hazard asked.

Utter only shrugged. 'If I don't float I'll sink.' And taking off his overcoat—they had acquired two fine coats in a hotel lobby— he crawled up to join his large black suitcase on top of the milk-wagon and flung himself down with arms outstretched, gripping the suitcase handle with his right hand.

Utter may have been beyond caring, but not so Hazard.

Surely it was, finally, his jealousy of me that made him submit to so reckless an undertaking. They were stopped on a high bank. Hazard dismounted from the wagon and led Girl (Utter had mistakenly given the gelding that name) down past windfalls and mudholes and tree-caught chunks of ice. Having found the way to open water, his feet wet and his trouser legs torn, he returned to his seat on the wagon; now he in turn stripped off his overcoat and jacket and handed them up to Utter.

'Are you ready?' Hazard called.

'I once screwed a Doukhobor girl who had taken off her clothes to object against the educational system,' Utter replied, clutching the handle of his suitcase. 'Doukhobor means spirit wrestler. It was for her I blew up the bridge.'

They drove into the main current, Hazard using a long pole to fend off floating trees and stumps and ice floes that were swept along by the hissing brown water. It is difficult to estimate the length of a river that winds and meanders as does the Cree, but I would guess that eighty miles downstream from this ford, or attempted fording, Hazard would have come to Wildfire Lake and his own deserted mansion. Instead, beneath the placidity of that soft spring sky, where a gull wheeled alone in its scavenging way (and gulls are seldom seen alone), Hazard, in the company of that wild man, risked life and limb. For the current did not rely on ice or snags to do its dirty work; by itself it turned the top-heavy wagon off its wheels. The wagon, on its side, floated; Hazard scrambled onto its new topside, only to find Utter leaning over the edge, still clinging to his large but now invisible suitcase. Their overcoats and Hazard's jacket were gone. Neither of them, strangely, made a sound or acknowledged the presence of the other. Girl kept his footing and strove heroically to pull the floating wagon to safety while the shafts, in turn, threatened to upset him into extinction.

'Cut that damned gelding loose and let him go,' Utter suddenly burst out.

'Not on your miserable life.'

'Fine.' Utter jerked his blond beard free from a wood splinter.

'Ah yes. I'll die with you. Take me down with you, you blind ambitious presumptuous fool.'

'Pitch off that damned fool suitcase,' Hazard replied.

'Not on your rotten trivial life.'

'Just let it go. We'll have another two inches of freeboard. At least then Girl—'

As easily as if the earth had dissolved into air beneath his feet, the struggling gelding was afloat.

'You stinking little pup with your defiance and your lust,' Utter said, one eye open. 'You snivelling nit. You act like a man in love. Your existence means nothing to the world. Mine means everything.'

'You're too damned heavy,' Hazard answered. 'Jump in.'

Utter only gripped his invisible suitcase the more desperately. 'I was not sent here for *this*.'

If both those men had drowned, how simply my life would have shone over their darkness. But I could wish no such fate upon Hazard. Even if he had already come to see me as his nameless rival, I could not wish him into that watery grave. As for Utter, however, with his windbag lies and foolish temptations, I might happily have mumbled a prayer over those engulfing ripples. They were impending death and he was their agent, I am certain.

Hazard saw the gelding was being swept along out of control by the wagon, swim as strongly as it might. Recklessly he leaped into the foam and the swirl, and swimming strongly himself he unhitched the traces that bound the gelding to a threatening doom. The wagon swung away and began to move faster.

'Jump!' Hazard shouted to Utter.

Utter, clown prince that he was, would not deign to move. Clinging grimly to the invisible handle he seemed to grip the water itself. 'And where to, you cock-peddling maniac? Ah yes, my good man. If the water doesn't drown me, the blocks of ice will grind me to death.'

There were indeed two very large and menacing blocks of ice being swept along behind them. An outhouse tilted crazily out of a bubble of mud, its deepset holes like two unmatched eyes.

'Jump! Jump!' On either side of the river the trees on the silent hills were as still as the lines in a Japanese drawing. The sun seemed to hesitate, red and savage, above the horizon. The river, icy cold, running faster now, was ominous and death-like, for not a bud or blossom had opened along its brown banks.

'I can't jump,' Utter called. 'Not into that balls-aching water.' His nose pulled down to the surface of the river he delivered nevertheless a farewell oration, not on his own behalf, but as a little memorial to Hazard. 'Watching you sputter and drown, I should jump in beside you? You brought me here, you tit. Ah yes. But I am quite content to witness your passage into the soggy depths without so much as batting an eye. I prefer dry socks and the sun on my neck. The question comes to mind: if I could by wetting one foot save your life, would I bother? Or is not the world better for your absence?'

At that moment, struck in the face by the hoof of a drowned pig, Hazard recalled the old Frenchwoman who had prophesied, '*La mer sera votre meurtrière.*'

'Would not,' Utter continued, 'that beautiful woman in Coulee Hill be happier for your untimely end? I notice even now that you are weaker than you were, you thresh with less determination. Poor moonface there in Coulee Hill will rejoice at the sad news. Your forehead is quite blue. Even your precious horse will no longer have to lug and pull you from place to place, as if—'

The floating wagon caught on the very tip-top of an underwater tree and was set to spinning like a barrel. Utter, likewise, spun into the brown and shitty foam.

He had forgotten his precious suitcase, I can tell you—when finally he bobbed sputtering and spitting to the surface. Hazard, unthinkingly, swam to the aid of the shrieking fool. But it was not Hazard who saved Utter. Rather it was the noble gelding that saved both men. Numb and fainting they clung one to his mane, one to his tail (it was Utter who clung to the latter), and Girl pulled them towards shore.

Just as their feet found the muddy bottom, a dozen or twenty jugs and bottles came floating by. Somewhere upstream an unfortunate moonshiner had not moved his camp in time. Utter tried to get hold of five bottles, only to lose all of them. Hazard, still clinging to Girl, managed to hook one finger into the handle on the neck of a one-gallon wine jug.

Shivering, exhausted, the two men crawled and staggered and flopped through the mud behind Girl; feebly they struggled to their feet; holding now to Girl's neck they were hauled through a heavily wooded coulee, the water rising at their very heels as if to suck them back into its dark depths. The sun, as if at a given signal, plunged below the horizon.

In the soft wash of darkness the two men made a final effort, both of them at the point of collapse. The horse stayed near the men, as if in sympathy; then they all together burst into a small clearing: and beheld a solid rectangular shadow before them. The reflections from a row of windows showed it to be a one-room school.

Utter collapsed onto the steps, panting and moaning, refusing to tamper with government property.

It was Hazard who found matches in the teacher's desk and lit a fire in the old stove. By its rosy glare he saw the absent children had pasted onto the windows cut-out shapes of Easter eggs and rabbits and purple and yellow tulips. The desks were set in neat rows facing the blackboard and the teacher's larger desk; the oiled floor had been swept spotlessly clean. In fact the only complaint Hazard could possibly make was that the woodbox had been left very nearly empty. Putting the last stick in the stove, he went to the door and asked Utter to bring in an armful.

Utter crawled in through the open door on his hands and knees and stretched out on the floor beside the hot stove.

'Damn you and your wedding.' Hazard took off his shoes to empty out the water, then put them back on. He watched, for three or four minutes, the shadowy flames on the mica windows in the stove's door; then he went outside. He took off his shirt and carefully he massaged the gelding dry.

Darkness came swiftly; the river a few hundred yards down the coulee pushed lumbering blocks of ice against the roots of resisting trees. Hazard, finishing the horse's legs, felt warm and exhausted and vital again; he forgot his irritation with Utter and went inside the school carrying a large armful of dry wood.

Utter, he found, had been imbibing from the jug without appreciable restraint.

'That stuff will kick like a mule,' Hazard said.

'I am free of the tyranny of love,' Utter announced.

Hazard hung his shirt to dry beside the stove and, picking up the jug, helped himself to a healthy snort.

'You are still not quite out of bondage,' Utter lamented. He rose up on one elbow. 'We need only some last little motion of the spirit to complete our journey.'

'We've got miles to go,' Hazard replied. In a peculiar snit he went flinging out through the door and slammed it. He checked Girl, tying him to a tree where he might find both protection from the night air and a little dead grass to nibble at. He was looking for the school pump when he noticed a flicker of light against the decorated school windows. But without giving it further thought he looked in vain for a pail; then he loaded his left arm with wood from the pile stacked neatly against the rear of the building.

As he pushed the door open with his foot, he saw the whole room was alight. Hazard dropped his armful of wood and leaped to grab the burning stick that Utter brandished as he ran almost dancing from the teacher's bookshelf to a cardboard globe. Utter, a huge man, was able to brush Hazard away like a fly, even at the same time flinging the stick into a dark far corner.

Frantically Hazard tried to save their only shelter, slapping at the flames with his wet shirt. But already the bright fire licked at the wall nearest the stove; when Hazard in desperation picked up the jug of moonshine and flung the last drop at the flames, he was already too late; he turned and found Utter missing.

The oiled floor became a bed of fire. Hazard's wet shirt was smoking now. Becoming dizzy and feeling his knees go weak, he flung himself towards the door.

Outside in the fluttering light of the conflagration Utter stood motionless with his arms folded mystically across his bare chest: he was as naked as a jaybird.

In a chapter that was seized by one of my doctors, I discussed at some length my theory of nakedness. If we are ever to achieve the ideals to which the more enlightened among us pay lip service, it strikes me we must first rid ourselves of an impulse towards hypocrisy and deceit and vanity and pretension and false pride. To achieve this end we must begin by freeing ourselves from clothing. I have surely done my bit; and yet I wish to avoid the kind of vanity that comes of being freed from vanity. Utter had not learned this lesson.

'I am doing this especially for you, Hazard Lepage,' Utter explained, pontifical and arrogant. 'You poor blind nut. You fart in a hailstorm. You peddler from hell. You ambitious ass. Now we must remedy the lover.'

'You'll freeze your balls off', Hazard said. 'Where are your pants ?'

Utter nodded stiffly toward the roof of the little school. His few clothes were already beginning to smoulder and smoke. 'I too once loved a strange woman.' Utter slapped his own bare but hairy chest very stoutly. 'I too, like you, have done homage. But we are free men at last; we are what that woman herself called *Svobodniki !*'

A mouse ran squeaking from the holocaust and darted at Utter, then turned and went blindly back into the flames.

I suspect that Hazard was in terror for his life; but he could not leave the poor nincompoop to freeze to death. Without hesitation he kept his pants on; and his shoes as well. He got as close to the fire as he dared, hoping to get warm one more time before the dark of night returned, and he very nearly singed his beard.

'*Svobodniki!*' Eugene Utter repeated, turning to warm his naked arse against the blazing school. 'Ah yes. At last we are free men.'

21

I have some bad news, my patient reader. The bald truth is, I have not the foggiest notion how the two men got out of their fix. The school was old and tinder-dry; in a few minutes it burned to the ground. The night was cold. Hazard refused to explain what happened next. I begged him in the interest of logic, of continuity, in the need to instruct and direct future generations, to give me a clue.

All I can say with certainty is this: they turned up at the wedding by 4 pm on Monday, 2 April, the two of them, dressed fit to kill in new suits, white shirts and expensive ties. Only Utter's shoes seemed to be out of keeping with the pervading spirit; they were in need of a shine and rather too large for his quite large feet.

Nicholas Melnyk had pitched a tent in the yard in front of his farmhouse. The square tent—I paced it off out of curiosity—was 54 feet by 54 feet. A dozen neighbouring men had worked hard to construct an excellent wooden floor. Thirty-odd women had meanwhile hustled and slaved for three days in the house, and in the out-of-doors at a row of stoves set up in the spring sunshine.

By 12 noon all was more than ready. A few minutes later the first of three cars, brilliant in crêpe paper streamers and garlands of flowers, roared tooting into the yard. Back from church of a sudden, the bridal party was heralded home by the cries of running children and the tears of the cooks, by the barking of dogs and the popping of corks. Whole columns of cars came following behind; they were parked in fields and pastures. Their occupants converged on the tent. The bride's father, scowling and proud, directed guests to their chairs; the mother fussed at veils and bouquets. But hardly had we finished lunch when we must dash off to Notikeewin to be lined up and made to grin and be photographed.

That frantic gesture was our last moment of calm; when we returned to the farm it was nearly 4 pm. Four hundred guests had assembled and most of them sat down in that huge tent to an absolutely immense reception dinner.

But why do I remember so well?

I caught my first glimpse of Hazard Lepage at that very moment. To be precise, we were supposedly praying: I could not resist looking up: across my table and beyond it, at the third table from mine, sat a man who had not bothered to wait for the prayers and toasts and greetings.

Little did I realize, staring greedily as I did at the bearded figure with the curly black hair and thick shoulders and great hatchet nose (not unlike my own) that I was looking at the subject of many years' study. On the contrary, all I saw was the man Martha had described to me, for she had told me of him often: and his dark penetrating eyes were not so gentle as she found them. His mouth which to her was sensuous was to me—his beard needed trimming—merely coarse. I happened to catch him eating a leg of turkey. He tore at the meat like a starved animal, all the while ignoring a kind lady who offered him a glass of water and a napkin.

I was not alone in regarding Hazard with surprise, for he seemed the dark shadow of the great blond ox who faced him across the table, his back to me. Utter had a bad cold which made him cough; he tipped up and guzzled from a bottle of whisky that stood before him in the middle of the table, spilling as he did so more than a little onto the lapels of his new blue suit.

I was myself dressed in black trousers and a white jacket complete with a carnation, as I was one of the three best men at my cousin's marriage to Catherine Melnyk. But, to say the least, I cannot remember what platitudes were offered in praise of both bride and groom. I do recall that when others raised their wine glasses, I raised mine. I smiled, no doubt, when I was supposed to smile. I trembled.

Hazard should have been horrified to understand that the bridegroom was my Uncle Tad's eldest son—and Uncle Tad found an excuse, before the eating commenced, to rise and speak.

'Okay, okay, folks,' were the words that caused Hazard to hesitate in his devouring of all that lay before him (and the women now had the tables completely set). Uncle Tad with a white handkerchief wiped the sweat from the top of his head. He leaned with one hand on his heavy cane. 'Tonight—' he shifted a wad of snuff in his lower lip—'even if our joy cannot equal the bridegroom's, at least we can celebrate in our own way.' He was vastly applauded for this insight but did not sit down. 'In a week my son goes off to war. He puts on, in seven days, the uniform of a soldier. What he takes off tonight is none of our business.' More laughter. More applause. 'I can only hope that he might honour the family—' He glanced sidelong at me.

I was wrestling with the question: Should I or should I not talk to Hazard when the opportunity presents itself? Should I introduce myself? Should I disguise my true identity?

But first we must eat. The speeches and toasts and applause were over. Uncle Tad had completed the awarding of his compliments and insults. Before us, for each six persons, stood a bottle of whisky and a bowl or dish or plate of each kind of food.

In the midst of all that extravagance I could only nibble at a shimmering jellied salad on one corner of my heaped plate. Meanwhile, by subtly straining and shifting, I was able to watch Hazard as he helped himself to tender fried chicken and more turkey; to thick slices of roast beef. I saw him ask about and then try the *holubci*—the steaming cabbage rolls; he took from the woman who was about to serve him the plate of cheese and potato dumplings with sour cream—*pyrohy*, I believe, is the name. He could not resist the sizzling steaks, the hamburgers smothered in onions, the sweet and sour, the variety of cold meats: God knows how many head of cattle and how many hogs had perished for the event. Dill pickles, sweet pickles, sour pickles, relish, tossed salad, cole slaw, johnny bread, biscuits and buns—no dish could pass Hazard's plate without being seized up and attacked. The bowls and platters seemed to skim back and forth along the tables: yet women began to refill them before they were empty. Someone had already tapped one of the six fat kegs that lay on trestles in a row by the door; waiters came with pitchers of beer and foam even while the guests tried to choose among varieties of cookies and cakes, date squares and brownies, pies and tarts and cheeses and candies and nuts and fruit.

I was truly sick with a kind of hunger. I nibbled at a date square, trying all the while to listen to the girl who chattered at my side. Indeed I believe she had baked the sweet I was supposed to sample. Then, in the confusion, as people finished eating and began to talk and drink (a group had started singing), I lost all track of Hazard and his friend.

I was of the bridal party; we had to be complimented and teased by hundreds of people, all of which I bore as gracefully as possibly I might. I helped myself to more wine. The smoke that hung in the huge tent was enough to dim the naked light bulbs and sear out one's eyes. Mr Melnyk was doling out cigars by the boxful. The noise turned every attempt at conversation into a sequence of hearty shouts. It seemed only a few minutes had gone by when the orchestra arrived. Men were moving tables out of the way. The players unpacked their instruments while six young fellows, much too drunk for their undertaking, manhandled a piano. Another eight hundred guests were arriving, for it was nine o'clock and time to dance. Where had the time gone? I asked myself . . .

Two large tables were left in one corner of the tent, buried under food and bottles. I was approaching one of those tables with the intention of refilling my wine glass when quite by accident Hazard and Uncle Tad and I all met at the same moment.

Each of us held an empty glass. Whatever I had planned to say to Hazard I could not at that moment utter, for my Uncle Tad beat me with a gruff shout. My own question was to have been quite simple and pointed: I had planned to approach with cold disdain and, looking down from my superior height, inquire: 'Are you then the infamous prick I fear you to be?' 'Dear old Hazard!' my Uncle Tad called out, though they stood not six inches apart. 'Hazard Lepage!' The smoke, I swear, made it difficult for us to see each other. 'Old hairy Hazard. Rehearsing for your own wedding, are you? Let me pour you a drink.'

Tad's manner was most deliberately insulting. I could never make much sense of his failure to understand Hazard, for Tad had started his career as a rustler. Tad told no one of his past; I only discovered this fragment from Old Lady Eshpeter in the course of doing my infinite research. It was a stallion that one night in the river hills smashed his right leg.

Before Hazard could answer the first question, Tad (while pouring) asked a second: 'Is Martha with you today?'

Hazard was sweating behind his beard. His eyes were ever so slightly glazed. He did not answer; rather, he turned and fled (or searched, he claimed to me later) through that swirling throng of people. Tad ignored my glass.

The bride and groom had completed the first dance. Now it was time for the bridal party to dance along with the newly-wed couple. We too went gliding onto the floor, the three women in pink and blue and yellow; we men each of us pressed and shaved and combed, wearing each of us a fresh carnation. I was dancing with the bride's younger sister. Was her name not Veronica? I believe it was. I believe, also, that she was not entirely bored with my moody presence; she yielded her young body so softly into my embrace.

It was my misfortune to be an abominable dancer. I was sweating with the pain of my embarrassment. Veronica, with one hand in mine, the other touching my neck, suggested directions and motions. But my long thin legs were not mine to command; they could not obey the impulses their awkwardness only confused.

When the third dance began, when the families of the fortunate couple waltzed onto the floor, I might have wept my relief. When the fourth began—when all that waiting mob burst onto the floor, forming into pairs, beginning to leap and plunge to a polka—I was only too relieved to be able to tell Veronica that I must retire to a bench and rest.

Hazard, meanwhile, was pushing and elbowing everywhere.

That he could not expect to find Martha I need not tell you, for she was in Coulee Hill, tending to her father's hotel. My absence was only tolerated by Uncle Timothy because I had been asked to serve as a best man. He himself disapproved violently of any early marriage, and he would not attend that of his nephew.

You must realize the temptation I experienced; I quite simply wanted to catch Hazard by the throat and talk with him, just to gauge the wit and confidence of my dear cousin's fiancé. But no, I would not allow myself the selfish luxury of further humiliating that drunk and misbehaving man. For Hazard and Utter, both of them indulging with unpardonable abandon, made excellent fools to the charming young couple so recently joined in wedlock.

I found Hazard—I could not resist at least looking for him—with a group of men around the beer kegs. They were all of them cracking lewd jokes, now and then breaking into a jig, each man alone. Eugene Utter especially was cutting up; with a mug of beer in each hand he concluded a jig by kicking high over Hazard's head.

'Like the fellow said,' Utter told his circle of admirers. 'I was just crazy to get married, but I didn't know it until after—' The crowd of men guffawed their appreciation. 'Ah yes,' Utter went on. 'Like my old man always told me—if a man gets married a second time, he didn't deserve to lose his first wife.' A waiter broke into our circle of laughing men with a pitcher of beer. Glasses were raised in various toasts. 'What's the fastest two-handed game in the world?' somebody wanted to know.

I find such talk offensive and did not linger further. In fact I did not again encounter Hazard until midnight, for I took pains not so much to find as to ignore him. I felt acute embarrassment for my poor absent Martha.

Then at midnight a long table was set up at the end of the tent in front of the orchestra. The bride and groom and bridal party stood behind the table; the guests lined up in what seemed an endless line to offer their congratulations and gifts. The frying pans and pillow cases and electric blankets were received by the bridesmaids and piled like so much treasure and booty in a shining heap behind the table; the cash was received on a plate and arranged into piles by none other than myself.

Married couples came drunk and laughing to the table; they gave their offerings; they received from the bride a piece of the huge wedding cake; they drank with the bride and groom an eloquent and heart-rousing toast. Tiberius, in the process of toasting a few hundred people, even though he had been cautioned only to wet his lips, was becoming quite drunk from so much wine; yet in all honour he could not let this show. In order to steady himself he took to hanging on to my collar with one finger, very nearly strangling me in the process. It was during this time that I looked up, purple in the face, sweating like a dog, to see Hazard and Utter approaching in the line.

A very ancient little old stooped man on the makeshift stage was playing a dulcimer; a number of older people had gathered around him to sing Ukrainian wedding songs. Thanks to them, what happened next went unnoticed.

For some reason I had arranged the stacks of money before me into five neat columns: the 50-dollar bills on my right, then the 20's to the left of that column, then the 10's, then the 5's, then the 1's—each column headed by a stack of five bills. I had in this fashion covered much of the table by the time Hazard staggered towards me; as he did so he reached to touch a pile of 20's—a breach of etiquette so abominable I blush to mention it even now. Utter was attempting to kiss the bride.

I was tired and cross by then, to be sure; in a little fit of impatience I rose up and pushed Hazard away from the table. Tiberius had me by the collar and restrained me at once, or I might in my impatience have demolished the misbehaving guest (if I might apply that term to one who was unbidden) right on the spot.

Tiberius, jovially, invited Hazard to share a toast with him. Unfortunately Hazard was too drunk to stumble up from where he had fallen; Utter, seeing his companion in this condition, swept him off the dirty floor and carried him like a sleeping child towards one of the exits.

We of the bridal party had earlier arranged that the bride and groom might depart from the merry-making at exactly 3 am.

It is, locally, a custom to interrupt, if possible, the young couple in their first night's pleasure. The origins of such a custom are lost in obscurity; I only wish I had time to expound upon a number of possible explanations. But Tiberius and Catherine were in something of a fix. They could not drive any great distance from the vicinity, for they were expected to be present at the next day's celebration to praise gifts, to eat again, and to dance again through the afternoon and evening, at which time they would finally be free to depart on a honeymoon—while those who remained behind would celebrate still further and clean up the mess on the third day.

As I say, the bride and groom were to depart at three, while the dancing would go on until sunrise. A shrewd groom, naturally, leaves a trail that is difficult to follow; Tiberius, as a son of his father, was nothing if not shrewd. By prior arrangement he and his bride slipped away from the tent unnoticed, on the pretext of joining a friend outside for a drink.

A few minutes later, three decorated cars went roaring out of the dark yard. They proved to be dragging tin cans; their hubcaps proved to be full of gravel; the noise alerted the rowdies who intended to badger the hapless groom.

I was myself in one of those fleeing cars with Veronica; in fact, we were the couple in the bridegroom's car. Thus, when the pranksters hurried to jump into their own cars and follow the groom, it was the car I drove that drew their mischief in its wake.

Veronica Melnyk, as I say, was with me; virginal and sweet though she was, she knew every trail and lane within ten miles of her father's farm; and indeed we led our tormentors on a chase they will surely never forget. By a deft and sudden turn on the one road in that vicinity that is not straight (because of a large slough), we directed two cars through a barbed wire fence and up to their headlights in water. Still another driver, not anticipating a correction line, became firmly stuck in a ditch full of croaking frogs and spring mud. The night rang richly to our daring. I concluded the escapade by driving straight away at seventy miles an hour down a rutted dirt road with the lights off.

Veronica clung to me in silence, only speaking now and then to suggest a new direction; she had a positive little genius for deceiving the scoundrels behind us. We found ourselves, finally, parked by a grain elevator in the town of New Galway. We sat listening with the engine turned off; all we could hear was our hearts beating. Satisfied that our pursuers had abandoned the pursuit, we were able to relax.

I turned the key in the ignition switch and stepped on the starter; the engine, idling softly, flooded the lavish interior with a soft warmth. I was suddenly too exhausted to drive on. Veronica, recognizing my condition, suggested we sit for a while.

Around us the town was either sound asleep or deserted; it was that darkest and sweetest part of the night, just before dawn. Veronica, who must have been as weary as I, put her head against my shoulder. She was a slim, frail creature; she seemed so helpless in her long gown that I put a protecting arm about her bare shoulders. In her gratitude she snuggled closer to me, responding warmly to my offer of security.

We were both quite simply spent from the chase. I said as much, and sweetly she reached up and grasped my left hand in both of hers. She was so careless in her exhaustion that, in taking my hand into her own, without design or subterfuge she rested it upon her bosom. Her breasts, I had earlier observed, while quite small, were not without a redeeming firmness and contour. She remarked that in my driving I had proved myself a brave man.

We sat nearly still in that awkward position for some considerable time, her forehead against my neck. When I moved my hand she did not stir, for she was seemingly asleep; I wanted to avoid in any way damaging her lovely bouquet of roses; she had spoken earlier of keeping it.

A pin, unfortunately, stuck me in the wrist as I groped to be careful. My motion brought Veronica's mouth up to my neck, an accident which I could not even then with any conviction deplore. However, feeling myself pricked by the pin, I said, quite naturally, 'Ouch!'

At that instant in the darkness a voice broke out from behind the front seat of the car; a figure gave an inarticulate cry as if stabbed or shot; and Veronica in turn let out such a scream of terror that I on occasion recall it to this day.

22

Hazard was later to tell me he was grateful I awakened him. He had wandered quite drunk (he insisted he was carried and then flung) into the back seat of the bridegroom's car. But in his sleep he was face to face with my Uncle Tad: and Tad had with him the most beautiful blue mare that Hazard had ever laid eyes on. The two men and the mare were in a tent; it was a flag-bedecked and gaudy circus tent rather than the neat box-like affair set up by Nicholas Melnyk to fête his daughter and son-in-law. The mare was standing in the centre of the centre ring.

Hazard, of course, was not as articulate as I might have wished in recalling the particulars of his terrible dream. I begged him to be more specific. He could only grunt and shake his head. Fortunately my own experience enabled me to flesh out the bones of his nearly dead memory: the fondest recollection of my own life has to do with a circus. As a very small child I was taken to one of those comic and exhilarating performances by my parents. They sat one on either side of me, and I was happy.

But Hazard argued: 'That old plug is lame,' he said to Tad. 'I wouldn't give you a wooden nickel for three of a kind.'

Tad touched the mare's belly with his cane and she began to trot in a circle around them, her haunches working like pistons. 'A horse of quality and substance,' he remarked.

'And blind or balky.'

'Okay, okay.' Tad was becoming just a little impatient. He

E

waved a hand in front of the mare's eyes. 'Do you see any blue there?'

Hazard looked; he found not the slightest sign of ophthalmia. 'She must have the heaves,' he commented.

Hazard always struck me as something of a hypochondriac: he was forever finding ailments where none existed. Tad assured him once more that the mare was up to snuff and then some; whereupon Hazard put his hands in his pockets and appeared about to leave. 'What're you asking?'

'I wasn't planning to sell,' Tad answered. 'You know my luck, if anybody does. I remember that day there in the Coulee Hill beer parlour, I traded horses nine times, working like a dog from ten in the morning till ten at night, and I ended up with the horse I started out with.'

In the shadows beyond the two men an invisible audience broke into a chuckle.

'And you only had a Model-A to boot,' Hazard called above the noise. 'What would twenty dollars look like, for a walking hat-rack like that one?'

'Like robbery,' Tad answered. He tapped his own bald head with his cane. 'The money isn't printed that will buy this mare.'

It was then Hazard knew he was in deep trouble. He told me that much, reticent as he was in discussing the hallucination that had afflicted him, and to assure him I burst out with an account of my own reassuring experience at the circus. I was supremely happy, nestled now against my father's arm, now against my mother's breast. The trumpet blared and the trapeze artists climbed their rope ladders into what seemed the very clouds. In my sweetest fear I pulled both my parents to me: and then for a wild moment the splendid figure of a man was floating free from his flying trapeze, somersaulting in the air—and as I started to scream his arms reached gently out, and swinging down from the sky came a girl so faithful and brave that all the crowd roared: and the man was caught and saved.

'So what are you asking?' Hazard replied to my Uncle Tad.

Tad gave a broad grin. 'Okay, okay. I'll tell you something,

Hazard. I want you to have this horse. I sincerely want you to have this horse. And I'm sure we can work out some arrangement that will be beneficial to both of us.' He tapped his cane on Hazard's arm. 'But how do I know you can handle her?'

Hazard with one leap was sitting astride the mare's back, both hands raised in the air to show he had no bridle or saddle.

The crowd gave a throaty shout of delight.

Hazard was a reckless man, God knows. He lacked the restraint that saves me from such folly. And folly it was, for Tad held in his hand a whip; he gave the whip a resounding crack.

'Do you agree to the following conditions?' Tad called from the centre of the ring.

'Yes sir,' Hazard said.

'You haven't heard them, you babbling fool.'

'No sir.'

The crowd in the shadows beyond the ring began to laugh and hoot. Tad swung the blacksnake and again it cracked like a breaking bone. 'According to the best of your knowledge and belief there is no affinity, consanguinity, or any other lawful cause or impediment, to bar or hinder the solemnization of the said marriage.'

'No sir,' Hazard said.

'And of course you know the degrees of affinity and consanguinity which, under the statutes in that behalf, bar the lawful solemnization of marriage.'

'No sir. Yes sir. I do not, sir.'

The blue mare, without bridle or saddle, seemed jittery; Hazard had to watch lest he lose his precarious seat. He was acutely aware of an invisible crowd awaiting his inevitable tumble.

'A man may not marry his,' Tad proceeded, his head nearly lost in the fatly curling wig of a judge, his eyes small and red, 'One: *grandmother*.'

'No sir.' The horse was trotting evenly now. 'She is not my grandmother,' Hazard enunciated precisely, able to breathe more easily now against the rhythm of the horse's body. 'My grandmother was not a virgin.'

'Okay.' Tad again raised his whip and the horse began to trot more rapidly. 'Two: *grandfather's wife.*'

'Ah yes.' Hazard carefully lifted his hands from the horse's mane. 'She loved bananas.'

'Three: *wife's grandmother.*'

'She lost her index finger.'

Tad gave his whip a crack: 'Four: *aunt.*'

A small gray fieldmouse stirred up from the sawdust on the floor of the ring.

'Bananas,' Hazard said. 'Wieners. Candles. Dill pickles. Coke bottles.'

Dear reader, is not all the past of mankind present there in the circus ring? Men must have trained a monkey to mock—to ape, I am tempted to write—his master, long before the first farmer hacked at the soil or tethered a cow. Surely a crow or parrot was taught to imitate his master's speech before even a chicken laid one egg to order. And just as surely, a crowd gathered to watch the mimicking monkey, the talking parrot or crow.

'Five,' Uncle Tad said. '*Uncle's wife.*'

A second mouse appeared.

'Six,' Uncle Tad said. '*Wife's aunt.*'

A third mouse, then a fourth, then a fifth, joined the first and second.

'Seven: *mother.*'

'But you see, sir,' Hazard explained, 'we were an island people. Abegweit, a Micmac word meaning: cradled on the waves. Isle St Jean. St John's Island. Prince Edward Island. It was Jacques Cartier himself who first observed, "It lacks only the nightingale."'

I should say that Hazard, in speaking to me of his mother, described her as a woman who was much obsessed with her Acadian background. Hazard's father was content to train horses for a wealthy doctor who was a consistent winner in the island's harness races, but his mother was given to meditating on the past. She was compulsively (I apologize for the word) drawn to that terrible year of 1758, when the Acadians of Isle St Jean, number-ing perhaps 3,500, were loaded onto boats by the English soldiers and scattered to other lands—except for the few who escaped capture, and the seven hundred who drowned. Her own family was one of those that escaped by hiding in the forest. I have searched old records and found that the names of the surviving families are given as Arsenault, Aucoin, Bernard, Blanchard, Blacquiere, Bourque, Buote, Cheverie, Chiasson, DesRoches, Doiron, Doucet, Gallant, Gaudet, Gauthier, LeBrun, Longueepee, LeClair, Martin . . . That is, you will note that Lepage is not among them.

'Eight: *step mother*.'

'There was a garden in the sea,' Hazard insisted. 'The soil red and rich. The sea abounding in oysters, clams, mackerel, cod, lobster, halibut, trout and salmon. It lacked only the night—'

A dozen mice rustled up out of the bones—I beg your pardon, the sawdust—and ran in a circle around first Tad on his stool, then Hazard on his horse, making a rough but dizzying kind of figure-eight. ('But Tad was standing,' I protested. 'He was on a stool,' Hazard replied.)

Incidentally, the Acadians of the island were three times plagued by mice before the Deportation. Hazard's mother herself was frightened half to death of the little creatures. I was vastly amused one morning to find one here in my tub.

'Nine: *wife's mother*.'

'She died of grief,' Hazard said. 'Or of childbirth.'

The whip cracked: 'Ten: *daughter*.'

'The soldiers, in loading the boats, quite carelessly separated families. *Mon pauvre soldat, inutile de te cacher*.'

My father, when I began to cry, called the balloon man and bought me not one but two balloons. The children about me were shouting and shrieking. I sat calm and still, the strings of the two balloons tugging as gently as kisses at my two small fists.

Hazard had not gone quite so deeply into the implications of his dreams as have I. For me, the dream of the circus, relived and repeated, amplified and explored, gave some little direction to each day's search. For instance, I learned that the good ship *Violet* foundered in a storm on its way across the Atlantic; the

Duke William exploded at sea. Thus there was some corroboration for his mother's remarks. The *Parnassus*, the *Narcissus* and the *Hind* were more successful.

Hazard, when I attempted to communicate to him my first awareness of the significance of his dream (and this was before I had commenced my very fruitful research), only guffawed. 'That old son of a bitch of a Tad,' he said, 'he told me he'd give me the mare for nothing if I promised never to have it bred. Figure that one out.'

Hazard also implied (as I understood him—and this is the one point where I neglected to make notes, having somehow lost my pencil) that the ultimate horror came at having, while standing on the back of the galloping horse, to leap through a ring of fire. The flaming circle blazed before his eyes like a hole in the darkness, waiting to swallow him down. He could neither leap at the bright circle nor jump from the back of the mare. The mice were a shrill hum at Tad's bare feet.

It was my startled cry that delivered the dreaming man. Veronica pulled away frantic from my side. Hazard was struggling with a door of the car, I reached and gave him a shove; I put the car into gear and stepped on the gas. We drove in considerable haste towards the Melnyk farm, Veronica and I, hardly speaking a word to each other until we were both safe inside her father's sheltering tent.

Incidentally, I have noticed one small point in my investigation of the laws governing marriage. You too will by now have remarked that nothing prevents one from entering into the bond of matrimony with one's first cousin. All the nasty little prejudices against that natural condition of mutual felicity are so much poppycock.

23

The lessons of history are manifold. If I have made nothing else clear, at least I have established that simple fact. One night

Hazard dreamed of being hounded and abused. His body motionless, he suffered in his mind only. Five days later he was reliving in only too physical a manner his nightmare of dread.

He slept for a while in the ditch in New Galway where I had deposited him with my impulsive shove; at dawn he staggered out past the feed mill on the edge of town and stopped at a filling station to ask directions to the Melnyk farm. The man on duty suggested a shortcut across a field three miles distant; it was while taking the shortcut that Hazard, walking through a grove of poplar, the grass white with hoarfrost, heard a horse whinny.

He recognized the whinny as that of Poseidon. Surely the farmer who had in error acquired the stallion was about to disappear forever. Hazard, in a panic, crouched down in the underbrush.

The man was coming into a small clearing; he was leading not one but two horses. Hazard had visions of seizing a mare with his stallion. He waited, gauging the man's location by the sound of footsteps: he sprang.

He drove his head into the man's midriff.

The grunt that resulted could belong to none other than Eugene Utter.

Utter, lying on the ground, looked up in great surprise. 'Ah yes,' he managed to say, getting his wind. 'What a sight for sore eyes. I've saved both Poesy and the gelding. You might show a little gratitude.'

Hazard only brushed the frost from a rock that was just then moving from the shade into the sun, and he sat down; he proceeded to tell his story of the night before. Utter, not a little spent and hungover, dozed off where he lay stretched out on the trail.

Hazard, talking on and on, recalling detail after detail, before long could hardly contain himself; he began to believe that the sheer horror of his nightmare was a good omen. Sitting on that cold stone in the warming sun, narrating and disputing to the sleeping figure of Utter, he found himself forced always back upon the same conclusion. Three times he started to say something else and yet announced: 'I have no choice but to get married without the slightest delay.'

As he contended with himself he quite by accident administered to Utter a swift kick in the side of the head. Utter, awakened, heard the argument as to why they should forsake the second day of the marriage festivities and depart at once for the hotel in Coulee Hill.

They decided to walk rather than ride. The gelding was not yet recovered from the previous escapade. Without further adieu, each man leading a horse, they found a dirt road and struck out directly for Martha's home.

Quite naturally, their wedding clothes soon became dusty and unkempt. Passing trucks more than once splattered the two men with mud. Their shoes and socks came to resemble the earth itself. But Utter had won ninety dollars in a poker game at the wedding; for three nights in succession they were able to sleep in small-town hotels, eat a hot meal towards evening, and consume a few beers before and after dining. Grudgingly, I must attribute at least this one virtue to Utter: on those rare occasions when he had something, he shared it with others.

On the fourth day, their sense of haste becoming more intense, they departed from the graded roads which tend to run either directly north and south or east and west. They turned in a south-easterly direction through the stretches of prairie and groves of poplar and unexpected slough holes that constitute the parklands. 'We'll steer by compass,' Utter announced, for the proposal was his. That night when the sun went down they were apparently lost. 'When it gets really dark,' Utter announced again, with his usual bravado, 'we'll be able to see the lights of a town somewhere near us.'

To make a long story short, when it got really dark they could see nothing but the darkness, for they had not between them so much as one match. All around, and all through the night, coyotes howled. They slept, in so far as they slept at all, on the floor of an empty granary, while a dozen mice dashed helter-skelter about them, hauling off the last few kernels of wheat.

It was a damp night as well; in the morning they were absolutely rigid with the cold. They began to run in circles around an old strawpile, all the while slapping their stiff arms like scarecrows in the wind. The discovery of the strawpile only made Hazard more miserable; in the straw they might have kept warm.

'To hell with it,' Hazard said. 'Let's go back the way we came.'

It was then Utter made another of his remarkable discoveries. He noticed, on the horizon, a column of thick black smoke.

This is the substance of human hope: a column of smoke on the farthest horizon. And all our faculties conspire to make of it the presence of our fellow men, the promise of a hot meal and a cheering fireside. By the time Hazard caught the two hobbled horses, the smoke had disappeared into the thickening fog. Utter insisted that rather than collapse from hunger and die of exposure, they ride Girl.

Thus it came about that they both mounted the chestnut gelding, the man in front holding the reins, the man in the rear leading Poseidon. 'Aim for that beacon,' Hazard instructed, pointing directly ahead at the blank wall of fog.

Utter, I suspect, simply gave the horse rein to go where it pleased. The horse plodded on, going straight through a brackish and shallow slough and into a grove of trees where Utter was very nearly knocked cold. Yet, after two hours, both men recognized the smell of burning rubber: 'Automobile tyres,' Utter announced. 'One time I helped blow up a car.'

The stench of burning rubber made Hazard recall his ride in the back of the car I drove on the night of the wedding (I had some difficulty releasing the brakes); he began to feel seasick. While there were no roads to be found anywhere, Utter began to argue that they were in the vicinity of a bad car accident and should turn away at once. The argument was settled quite as suddenly as it began: three yelping coyotes materialized out of the fog and ran directly under the hoofs of the two horses, one of the coyotes bleeding badly and trailing a yard or two of intestine. Four shots rang out distantly, muffled on the fog.

Only then did Hazard realize that a coyote hunt was in progress.

Shells had become so scarce because of the war that coyotes had multiplied into great abundance. In spring, receiving an allowance of ammunition from the government, a group of young men would surround an area that was approximately ten miles in diameter; someone would light a large fire in the middle to act as a beacon and the hunters would begin to walk towards it, gradually driving the surrounded coyotes into a smaller and smaller and ever-closing circle, whereupon the frantic animals were shot or at least shot at with shotguns amidst great excitement and hilarity.

I know the details of this particular hunt because I was asked to participate and declined. I have no stomach whatsoever for killing. And I had already been too much absent from the hotel and Martha.

I was invited to participate by Tad Proudfoot's four smirking younger sons; they were all well equipped with lethal weapons and they delighted in anything that enabled them to pretend at waging war.

Hazard and Utter, when a charge of buckshot whizzed hardly a foot above their heads, both tumbled from the gelding's back as if shot; perhaps the horse started; they were riding bareback. Hazard was so foolish as to remount the gelding, leading the stallion. Utter, on the other hand, having been sought too often by the RCMP and other representatives of justice, chose to run just as hard as he could, crouched, you might say, as if he had his tail between his legs.

As I shall explain later, he quickly found himself outside the ring of fire. Further, he stumbled upon an automobile loaded with three extra shotguns and considerable extra ammunition. In a matter of minutes he was able to start the car, thanks to having once loved a Doukhobor girl. He promptly drove away, and as it turned out he drove directly to Hazard's mansion (which he had often heard described) and waited a full week for Hazard before finally giving up the wait and driving on; let it be added—with Tad Proudfoot's new Buick and three bottles of very expensive whisky.

Hazard made the error of trying to outrun the hunters, perhaps because of his reluctance to be turned from a path that led directly towards Martha. Indeed, it seems to me that if Utter had most sincerely intended to rejoin Hazard, he should himself have gone to Coulee Hill.

The countryside south-west of that town is sandy with some hardpan; it is more suited to ranching than to farming, and as a consequence is mostly open range rather than fenced and tilled fields. I believe the area was once a shallow lake, but it was quickly drained by early settlers. Hazard, riding hard, was encumbered by having to lead Poseidon through a patch of wolf willow. The scrub bushes must have offered the illusion of protection to more than one animal. Poseidon shied most grievously when another coyote came loping out of the fog, only to be shot dead right under Girl's nose.

Everywhere about the lone rider the visible air rang with the cries of gun-happy and young but invisible hunters; they might have been so many spirits and ghosts. But the bang and whine were enough to make poor Hazard recall his own youthful days in the trenches of France. He bent low over the gelding's mane and gave a stout kick with both heels.

At that moment the hunters behind him ran directly onto the hunters on the far side of the circle; an impudent fortune now sent Hazard galloping down upon four young men who were having the time of their lives. He was close enough to recognize them as none other than Thatcher, Toreador, Tennyson and Titmarsh Proudfoot. They levelled their arsenal of guns as if they had been a firing squad.

It has often struck me that in the act of naming we distinguish ourselves from the other unfortunate animals with whom we share this planet. They seem under no necessity to deny the fact that we are all, so to speak, one; that each of us is, possibly, everyone else . . .

But I must not indulge myself: the Proudfoot boys, four snivelling little bastards that they were, did not in turn recognize Hazard. Rather, yielding to a romantic impulse that had already gone quite mad, they decided (or pretended) they had hit upon the culprit who had recently been guilty of the vicious crime of burglary.

Tiberius and his new wife Catherine on the night of their wedding stayed in Notikeewin with an old maid, one of the many Burkhardt women. Before going to the old maid's house, however, Tiberius discreetly parked his borrowed and decorated car behind the John Backstrom MLA Funeral Parlour. It was then he noticed that the old house had been broken into through the back door.

I do not for a moment believe that Hazard and Utter forced their way into that building; the point at which they crossed the Cree River is fourteen miles from the city of Notikeewin. I cannot imagine that Utter walked or rode those fourteen miles stark naked in search of clothing, least of all the clothing intended for the dead. Further, the owner of the funeral home, decorated for bravery at Dieppe where he lost thirty men but blew up a bridge, had been away for nearly five years, his wife and daughter packed off to board with relatives. The place, all locked up and deserted, could have been burglarized at any time over that period.

But let us return to the incident at hand: the horse that Hazard rode was shot dead from under him, a bullet through its neck. Poor old Girl had not time to say please or thank you before rolling in the dust. Hazard flung himself clear just in time to avoid being crushed. In the process he let go of the halter rope and Poseidon nearly escaped. But Hazard rose to his knees, dived to catch the frightened beast—and while kneeling in the consequent awkward position he himself received from some invisible gunman the full force of a discharged shotgun shell.

Hazard had been shot in the posterior region of his anatomy. 'I was hit square in the arse,' was his way of putting it.

Indeed, bleeding profusely, he cried out for help: only to find that now the noise and racket had retreated from the vicinity as rapidly as they had first appeared. 'Utter,' he called one last time. The silence engulfed him.

What a strange conclusion that would have been, for a man who

116

once lamented to Martha that even in a prairie beer parlour he could on occasion smell the salt tang of the sea. I have investigated various sources that might lead me to an understanding of that man and the brine from which, some would argue, we all issued; puzzling as it is, my sources indicate that the Lepages were a Rimouski family. Their seigneury was established on the shores of the St Lawrence in 1660; their coat of arms consists of a black eagle on a silver shield: *'un écu blanc (argent) portant en son milieu un aigle noir (sable) dont les griffes, le bec et les éperons sont rouges (gueules).'* Further, one branch of the family has added the motto in English: NOTHING IN MODERATION. All indications are that the Lepages of Rimouski were great dreamers about the future: *cette mauvaise habitude qui sépare les Française des Anglais.*

Hazard must then have been one of them; his dream might have ended right that morning, had he not heard a new voice crying in the blanket of what now had become a fog of the most incredible whiteness. It was a feminine voice, distant and beautiful.

Hazard was able to halloo feebly. The voice answered. Using all his remaining strength to stand up erect and breathe deeply, he hallooed again.

'Halloo,' came the answer.

He feared for a moment it was an echo. But the distant voice was beautiful and reassuring on the enshrouding fog.

'Halloooo,' he called.

'Halloooo.'

'Halloooooo.'

'Halloooooo.'

And then he tried one more time: 'Halloooooooo.'

There was no answer. Hazard began to feel dizzy and weak. He—the heroism of the man knew no bounds—pulled Poseidon to him, for he wished with his final strength to take the halter from the stallion's head and turn him completely free. He struggled with the buckle. Then his knees threatened to give and he used the stallion's mane to hold himself upright, the blood running freely and warm down the backs of his chilling legs. The stickiness was vaguely irritating. But the horse must be free—

'Who do you think you are?' a voice demanded.

Hazard turned from Poseidon to face into the barrel of a rifle. The zero of steel at the barrel's end seemed large enough to swallow him. His gaze swam away and he was next able to make out a palomino mare, then a brown riding boot complete with a bloodied spur, then an ornate saddle.

He looked up against the blinding white glare of the fog.

Before his eyes, bending down out of the mist, came a face, a vision of such stunning beauty and youth that Hazard could only give an inarticulate groan of despair. The woman's black hair had been tossed free of its binding by the motion of her galloping horse; a light dew glistened on the loosened strands. The woman's cheek, touched pink by the gallop, had apparently been whipped and cut by an unseen branch. Haughty and challenging, two eyes, larger and darker than Hazard's own, watched in a moment of wary stillness, then flashed in anger: 'I want no hunting on my land.'

Hazard did not answer. A blue stallion leaped through his mind. He pitched forward on his bearded white face onto the fresh mound of earth beside a gopher hole.

24

To elaborate further on what I was saying about names—I have more than once remarked that the pleasure in listening to a hockey game, as I do each Saturday night during the long winter, resides not only in the air of suppressed and yet impending violence, but also in the rain upon our senses of those sudden and glamorous names . . . Mikita from the corner for the Black Hawks. A backhander by Laperriere. Kelly upended by Marshall. In for the puck goes Bobby Hull. Here is Delvecchio faking a shot . . . I sit contented in my clean white tub, the radio turned low, square and protective on the windowsill, glossy against the dark night beyond. I close my eyes against the books and notes and cards and papers heaped about and upon me. My dull task is itself buried in my name-horde . . . those forever youthful names like Terry Sawchuk and Glenn Hall. Gordie Howe. Pierre Pilote. Stemkowski and Horton of the Leafs. My Rousseau plays right wing. Here is Ullman for Detroit; he blocks the pass. Ferguson entering the penalty box, two minutes for interference. Ed Giacomin makes the save. Pulford's slap shot is high. Those children of winter are my dream: they race in the night's dead hours. Uniforms identify the enemy, the friend. Each man guards his place. When you are struck, you strike back. Bobby Orr steps into Keon. J. C. Tremblay knocked down by Van Impe. Wharram is now on the ice. A penalty for slashing to Harper of Montreal. Esposito tries to centre it. Geoffrion holds it against the boards. Bucyk up the boards and Mohns chasing it. They're hitting the corners on DeJordy tonight. Conacher driving in . . . Do they see themselves in the gashed ice? Angotti. Nestorenko. Jean Belliveau and Jim Pappin. They must welcome the comforting fall of snow. Pit Martin of the Bruins. Gilbert of New York. Rogatien Vachon. Pronovost. Eddie Shack. Henri Richard and Harry Howell. Johnny Bower covering up. The Red Wings keep the pressure on . . . O how we hate to see spring come to this land.

The name Eshpeter is another of those startling and beautiful names.

The Eshpeter Ranch is a big one for that area; it occupies twelve sections. Marie Eshpeter managed the whole spread alone, for her father was dead, her old mother was nearly completely blind. Her only brother, serving under Lt John Backstrom, was taken prisoner at Dieppe and a few months later was killed while attempting to escape.

It was on the Eshpeter Ranch that I talked for so many afternoon hours and warm spring days with Hazard Lepage. Looking back now, I realize he was glad to chat with me, though at the time he often seemed gruff and impatient. One time in my callous youthfulness I dared ask if he wasn't stretching a point; 'You tell it,' he said, 'if you know better.'

But mostly he joked and laughed, and laughing is not easy for a man condemned to lie for days on his stomach.

I should interject that while Marie Eshpeter and Martha Proudfoot were by no means friends, they were acquainted. Martha had a few times pastured her horses on the Eshpeter place for the driest part of the summer, and hoped to do so again that coming August. Indeed, it was my going on an errand out to the ranch (it was hardly ten miles from Coulee Hill) that led to my discovering Hazard's whereabouts.

Why I did not tell Martha of my discovery, I hope to make quite plain and obvious. At any rate, in a very short time I was visiting the Eshpeters so often that Martha one evening upon my late return accused me of being in love with Marie. 'Remember, her beauty is exceeded only by her aloofness,' Martha said with a smile. But the joking manner did not for a moment conceal her genuine concern, her possessiveness, I might add.

Little did she realize that I was making my visits on her behalf, for we must now examine Hazard's own charge that Marie Eshpeter cast a spell upon him. On the validity of his assertion rests our judgment of the man's unlikely behaviour.

Granted he was very seriously wounded; or to quote Hazard again, 'My arse looked like a colander.' But his complaint that he was unable to escape her presence rests not upon the condition of his backside, but on the potency of her magic. 'I'm in her clutches,' Hazard once remarked to me, half musing, half as an aside.

Rumour had long held that Old Lady Eshpeter was a witch of some sort. My investigation into the events recounted to me by others, along with my own remarkable experiences, leads me to suspect the presence of nothing other than a poltergeist.

The initial difficulty was this: Hazard could not lie upon his back, and therefore must lie upon his belly. Marie nursed him. As beautiful as she was, she was also the picture of physical fitness; the discovery was soon made that while Hazard could neither sit, stand nor turn over, he could lie upon her belly as well as on his own.

That Hazard did heal so slowly is one of the medical peculiarities of the case. He lay baby-like upon Marie's full breasts, upon her milk-white thighs; instead of appearing to improve, he seemed forever to be on the verge of a relapse. Hours became days, the days weeks. His recovery was to say the least, tardy. Not that he complained. On the contrary, he was exceptionally submissive to his suffering. It was this very flagging of his rebellious spirit that came finally to worry me.

On three occasions during the first few weeks of Hazard's convalescence I had occasion to stay overnight on the Eshpeter Ranch: the first time was the result of bad roads. The spring thaw had made the roads very soft, but a week or so after my first shock at discovering Hazard's condition I could not resist: I drove out to the ranch in the second of my Uncle Timothy's autos, simply to talk for a while with the ailing patient.

Hazard spent the afternoon on a sunporch, stretched out flat on a mattress on the floor, sometimes with apology exposing his extensive injury to the salubrious effects of sunlight. I sat in a rocking chair at his side, and in my eagerness to understand him completely began on that particular occasion to take extensive notes on his past. Not trusting to memory, I borrowed paper and a pencil from the blind old lady who hovered constantly in the shadowy rooms beyond us. I made no secret of the fact that I had just recently—it happened a day or two after Tiberius Proudfoot's wedding—conceived the notion that I would write a few years hence a novel; Hazard was, I believe, flattered at the prospect of becoming a fictitious character. I at the time imagined I would write a wonderfully eloquent love story; indeed, anything but a biography.

When evening came, I was told by one of the hired men (Marie employed three) that during the day two cattle trucks had made the road nearly impassable. Without further ado I agreed (perhaps I even suggested) that I should stay overnight.

The Eshpeter house is a big rambling affair that grew without design or even very much purpose; it lacks the deliberate, stern proportions of Hazard's mansion. I was given a room on the third floor in what was simply a glorified attic. I am not especially frightened of the dark, but height and darkness put together, along with the moaning of the prairie wind, do make me at least susceptible to uneasiness. Marie served an excellent if modest supper, then retired to care for the needs of Hazard; I was left in the company of Old Lady Eshpeter.

Because she was so very nearly blind, she neglected to light any lamps; we talked in the growing dusk, she and I; she was very much interested in the recent increase in the number of owls. I had not noticed it myself, but I explained that mice first of all increase in number, then owls do likewise. I used the expressions 'balance of nature' and 'compensation'. What form of compensation develops, she wanted to know, when one goes blind? I tried to be jovial about the matter. What happens, I countered, when love is not reciprocated? It was her turn to chuckle, in so far as the noise that came from her long throat might be called a chuckle at all. But a good deal of the time we sat in absolute silence, listening to the sounds from outside the house: cattle lowing in a feed lot, a dog barking at its shadow. A cat scratching at the screen door. A horse pawing the floor in one of the distant barns.

This Eshpeter spread is three miles from the nearest neighbour and so located that in every direction you see, if you can bring yourself to look, a slightly heaving stretch of fields and pastures that seems to end or dissolve where the sky begins. Perhaps the unlit room was to be preferred to the out-of-doors. But when darkness threatened to envelop even the dark shadow that was the old lady, I asked if I might be shown to my bed. Thus it came about that the old lady and not her daughter showed me to the attic room. I should have asked for a coal oil lamp; but to ask would have been to remind her of her unfortunate condition. And I found myself shy in that little bedroom with the old woman.

Alone, I undressed by the pale thin moonlight that came through my only window. My body, so eerily white, was at first all I could see in the shadows. It was, I must confess, momentarily exciting to stand alone in that pool of darkness quite nude. Then I was able to make out beside the cast iron bed a low stand, and on it a basin, a pitcher of water, and a solid old earthenware cup of the kind found in small-town restaurants.

I first became aware of the rappings when I tried to sleep; and at first I assumed it must be a bird on the roof directly above me. I even wondered if it might be one of Mrs Eshpeter's countless owls. But, listening carefully, I soon realized the noise was not so much on the roof as in one of the walls about me, though I could not, concentrate as I might, determine which wall. I put my head under the pillow for a good while, but to no avail. Then I turned over and lay on my back: I focused all my powers of perception on one of the four walls that angled over me. Immediately the sound shifted to an adjoining wall. I shifted my attention to that wall, staring so hard I must pierce the very darkness. The sound shifted again: but always it was a monotonous, regular, insistent knock knock knock knock knock knock knock knock. Having no pyjamas, I found myself becoming somewhat chilly; the chilliness only gave assurance that I should not escape into sleep.

Finally the tapping was not to be endured by mortal man. I sat up and swung my legs over the side of the sagging deep bed: and it was then the cup sailed visibly before my eyes across the room and crashed through one of the four panes that made up my only window.

While I was not struck into terror, I did leap from the bed and flee in considerable haste down the narrow steep stairway to the floor below. I was greeted at the bottom of the stairs by Marie herself, dressed in the flimsiest nightgown and carrying a coal oil lamp.

'What is it?' she inquired.

What could I say? Suddenly the house was very quiet. I did not want to embarrass her about the rappings; yet I had a broken window to account for. 'A cup,' I said, matter of factly, 'flew across my room and broke one of your windows.'

'One of the men can repair it in the morning,' she said.

Can you imagine such utter calm in the face of the supernatural? But she faced me down without a smile. Not to be outdone, I let just the hint of a smile cross my face.

'Excellent,' I said.

'Would you like a glass of orange juice?' she inquired.

'I'm fine,' I said. I found myself beginning to shiver. Turning, I fled again; this time back up the stairway. But even in my haste I saw that she too turned away—and went directly to Hazard's room.

The second occasion of my staying overnight was of a different sort, and quite— But let me interrupt in order to explain.

The very process of recurrence is what enables us to learn, to improve, to correct past errors, to understand the present, to guide the generations that are to come. Yet it is precisely this same characteristic of life that makes life unendurable. Men of more experience than I have lamented at the repetitious nature of the ultimate creative act itself. It is only by a mastery of the process of *repetition* (you will note the repeated 'e', the 't' and the 'i', and the 'tit' standing out boldly in the middle) that we can learn to endure; yet we can only master the process by a lifetime of repetition. Many, I suspect, are tempted to despair. But I have sought other solutions and, I might add, with no little success. The path that would appear to lead to madness is surely the high-road to art. If someone chooses to do a study of my life, he will proffer an exemplum to mankind. The recognition of the basic predicament, for instance, enabled me with ease to give up smoking.

But as I say, I left the Eshpeter residence with a resolve never again to stay overnight; two weeks later I quite by accident ran out of gas just when I had driven one mile on my way home. I had no choice but to walk back and ask that I be given shelter until morning.

Strangely enough, I was pleased to be offered the same tiny attic room, for after my initial shock I had slept like a baby.

I had by this time, in the course of three or four recent afternoon visits, established beyond all doubt the nature of the relationship between Hazard and Marie. One would have had to be blind not to guess what was going on. She was spoken of in town, when mentioned at all, as a painfully shy woman; obviously, with Hazard, she had become brazen beyond every bound of decency. Hazard, confined as he was to a peculiar inactivity by the nature of his wound, had aroused in the woman every imaginable kind of inventiveness and improvisation in order that the two of them might be carnally satisfied. The hired men were out in the fields fixing fence or sowing a little grain or caring for the spring calves; Mrs Eshpeter was in the kitchen preparing meals, working not from sight but from memory. Hazard and Marie gave rein to their every fantasy, translating all into fact.

Alone in my attic room, I could not help that night but hear their low voices, their secretive laughter: I must confess, even the squeaking and groaning of the firm old bed on which Hazard was supposedly recuperating. I did fall asleep, however, after a very long time; only to be disturbed by the pillow's moving from under my head. In my drowsiness I merely searched for it in the dark and replaced it where it belonged. This happened a second time; again I found it and replaced it.

Then it was of a sudden violently snatched away: I leaped up and grabbed at whosoever was tormenting me—only to find I was absolutely alone in the room. I say this with confidence because I very deliberately and coolly and carefully felt my way around the walls. The only sound now was that of the prairie wind on the dormer. Again I returned to bed and to sleep.

I was awakened one last time, and this time I was not likely to fall asleep again: the bed shook and shuddered beneath me. In my fright I clutched at the pillow which had earlier eluded me; but now the upper left iron post of the bed began to rise; even as the bed rose it continued to shake; the pillow and I were flung bodily onto the floor.

It was the thump of my falling that this time brought Marie up the narrow stairs to my little room. Again she carried a lamp. And this time she wore nothing but her brassiere and the thinnest kind of panties; as she bent over me I was aware of the outline of her full breasts; I could recognize even the contour if not the colour of her engorged nipples. If I might say so, one was also aware of the pubic hairs pressing through the pale white undergarment.

'I have brought you a candle,' she said.

With that she lit a candle by lifting the globe from her coal oil lamp, and carefully she placed the lit candle on the stand beside my bed. It was, I could tell at a glance, a short fat candle of the kind found in a number of churches. The broken pane in my only window had not in fact been replaced; the flame, caught in the draught, sent shadows crazily to pattern the walls.

We Proudfoots are surely not of a religious persuasion that places faith in blest candles; yet, a moment or two after Marie's departure, I simply lapsed, right there on the floor all tangled in blankets and sheets, my hands folded across my naked chest, into the most profound sleep I have ever experienced.

Only later was I to suspect that Marie herself rather than her mother was the controlling force behind the presence of the poltergeist. Listening to the gossip of men in the beer parlour (while I was too young myself legally to drink, Uncle Tim quite often let me serve the customers) I learned of other events that had occurred on the Eshpeter place over the past few years. I revealed none of the harrassment I had experienced, however; I merely listened. It seems that on one occasion a visiting cattle buyer had seen a sausage (in the retelling it became a serpent) climbing a ladder beneath a window of the large house; he paid a ridiculously high price for the cattle he had been dickering for with the old lady and skinned out with no further comment. On another occasion a man who went out to sell brushes was in the kitchen, bent over his suitcase, when a butcher knife sailed through the air and pierced his hat where it lay on the kitchen table. Still another fellow, intent on scotching these rumours, went out past the woodpile towards the outhouse—he found himself somewhat nervous—and noticed beside the path a pile of discarded bones: he thought nothing of them until they stood up. Only once did I hear a loafer in the beer parlour speculate that Marie herself (not the old woman) had got these powers by reading the Book of Moses backwards—a book which I have not yet had the opportunity to peruse.

I would not for the world have stayed another night in that house; yet I was under some necessity to visit Hazard occasionally (my notes were piling up at a wonderful rate), and I did so.

At this time Martha and I were achieving some equilibrium in the see-saw varieties of our intimacy; she had recently permitted me to enter her room and talk with her nightly while she prepared for bed. For this reason alone I should surely not have stayed on the Eshpeter Ranch past the middle of the afternoon.

But one day in the early part of July I was caught out there by a fearful thunderstorm. It had been a hot muggy day; Hazard was improved enough to sit up; he and I had sat most of the afternoon on the sunporch while I scribbled and he talked and drank the case of beer I had—should we say, smuggled—from my uncle's icehouse.

It was on this occasion that I reasoned most emphatically with Hazard.

'The season for breeding horses,' I suggested, 'will soon be over.'

'It'll last another month,' he said.

'But you haven't found a recipient,' I said.

I made this remark deliberately, for Marie had on her ranch a number of fine saddle horses. I was curious to know if any one of them might shortly be bred. Hazard was sitting on an inflated car tyre on a rocking chair. 'I may postpone my plans for a year,' he announced casually.

'Next year,' I burst out, 'will be worse, surely.'

Hazard laughed briefly but heartily. 'Next year Marie will be able to spare one of her younger mares. She promised me—'

Just then the first clap of thunder struck. The storm was coming up from behind the house and we had not noticed its arrival. We both stopped talking; in a moment the sky darkened.

'You better strike out for home,' Hazard said, 'or you won't make it. That gumbo road will be like a greased pole.'

Hazard had recently begun to drive the old Eshpeter car under

127

Marie's guidance, and had come to affect a certain authority. It was one of their pleasures to drive of a morning out onto the beautiful open grasslands, Hazard perched cockily on his tyre, and loll away a few hours in a sunny hollow or ravine. The grinning idiot had one afternoon greeted me with his beard festooned with the small beaked flowers of the shooting star.

'I'll run say good-bye to Marie,' I said.

In something of a hurry I ran out to where she was supervising the day's activities. I found her in the second of three big barns; and, rushed as I was for time, I stopped motionless. She was in a stall combing down Hazard's stallion. She spoke softly to the great blue beast, running the iron comb through his mane, and he whinnied nervously. But her hands touched his flanks, his belly; and to my surprise he was calmed.

It was then I dared speak. 'I'll be going now, Marie,' I said.

Marie gave a start. Then she saw me in the half-light of the barn. 'O,' she said. 'I'll see you to your car.'

At the door of the barn we saw drops of rain kicking up the powdered dust. The barns are a good ways from the house. We began walking side by side.

'Do you keep many bones around the place?' I inquired casually.

'Bones?' Her attempt at indifference nearly failed her, for I took her rather by surprise.

'Bones,' I insisted.

'Bones,' she repeated.

'Yes,' I said. 'You know. Bones.' Really, I did not want to provoke the woman. In her presence at that moment I was free of all fear. I might calmly have faced a whole yard full of rising bones.

'What kind of bones did you have in mind?' she asked.

Then we saw we had to run; she took me by the hand and we ran as fast as we might; but the rain was faster. The great racing cold drops pelted us.

When we got to the porch we were both soaking wet. Marie's dress clung to her beautiful hard body; it was then I recognized she had on not a single item of underclothing beneath the light cotton dress. But she did not care one iota; she only laughed when Hazard patted the full outline of her wet buttocks.

'Will you have a drink?' she asked, both to Hazard and to me.

For some reason, while I seldom indulge, I agreed that I would. She brought out from inside the house a bottle of rye and three empty glasses and a pitcher of water; she still had not bothered to take off her soaked dress. And, as usual when Marie was present, the old lady avoided us.

That night I went to bed quite dizzy, otherwise I would not have been able to face the prospect of the attic room. As it was, I made my way up the narrow staircase quite alone. Thunder continued to crash and roar about my head, as if I had mounted into the clouds; but I was defiant. I undressed in that dark room, not giving a damn; when I could not find the basin I waited for lightning, and in the sudden blue glow I found what I sought and rinsed my face and arms and chest and private parts in clear cold water.

It was the silence that awakened me. The storm had passed, and just as suddenly both the wind and the thunder were gone. I awakened into the pitch black of that moonless night: I wanted badly to scream but could not get a squeak out of my throat.

My mouth was full of pins.

My mouth was full of safety pins of the size you might use on a diaper. I spat them out; I knocked them out of my mouth with my groping fingers. I fled in the absolute darkness down the narrow stairway and ran for dear life directly to Hazard's room.

I burst into the room without giving so much as one knock or a single halloo: a candle burned on a small table before the window; it had burned so low in its saucer the flame was hardly more than a sputtering glow. I could not see clearly in that faint light, but a tall thin (it looked like wax) statue of something or other reflected the candle's glow and I am certain of what I saw: they were both of them, Hazard and Marie, on the far side of the high old bed—they were both down on their hands and knees. And they did not see me, for Marie was faced away, her lovely full buttocks towards me, crystal smooth in the pale light, bathed in the thinnest gloss of sweat, a gentle arrow of black engaging my eyes where Hazard touched his bearded face to her flesh and nipped at her thigh.

'Hazard?' I whispered, not daring to think or consider.

I swear before God and man that he whinnied.

I need hardly add that I fainted dead away right there on the spot.

25

It strikes me that I have been remiss in describing, not this perverse human caricature of the essential animal, but that animal itself. Let me make amends, my dear reader; and I can best describe Poseidon by referring you to the superlative grace and beauty of Chinese art.

I hardly know where to suggest you begin. Those old Chinese artists: they drew their horses true to life, true to the rhythm of life. They dreamed their horses and made the horse too. They had their living dream of horses . . . Ah, where to begin? Why is the truth never where it should be? Is the truth of the man in the man or in his biography? Is the truth of the beast in the flesh and confusion or in the few skilfully arranged lines . . . You might see the bronze horses of the Late Chou Dynasty. Or 'The Five Horses' of Li Lung-mien, that lovely ink drawing on, if I recall correctly, a handscroll. Or by all means spend an hour contemplating the horses of Chao Meng-fu as they go to their watering. . . . Yet for all these exquisite examples, I myself am always drawn to the T'ang Dynasty. At one time in the China of T'ai-tsung there were forty thousand horses in the Imperial stables. Can you imagine . . . But study for one day that one horse—Han Kang's bold creation, Shining Light of the Night. O for the mad extravagance of that lost violent dynasty. Even to the grave they sent a man with mortuary horses. That perfect porcelain, those figurines for the tomb, those grave-goods with a finely crackled glaze, those horses for the spirit, brown or yellow, or even a gentle green, and ever so rarely—the softest blue . . . Our pitiful world: we pack a corpse off in copper and steel that it might for an extra year bewilder the dust. And yet one horse for the spirit's night and we would be immortal—

The mind wanders. What a strange expression. But when I awoke to the porcelain blue of dawn, Hazard was sitting fully dressed in a chair beside my bed. *His bed*, I should say, for now I was in his bed: and though naked I was covered over with a heap of blankets, and quilts.

'Feeling a bit better, young fellow?' Hazard asked.

I assured him that I was in excellent condition.

'You gave me a bit of a scare,' he said.

I should guess I did.

'I'll tell you, boy,' he went on, patting my forehead (I realized I had been sweating like a pig under all those covers), 'that bed would restore a bale of hay to its original vigour. Just sleep there one night, and you wake up hornier than a two-peckered goat.'

When the door opened, Marie's mother came in. Bent over a tray of bacon and eggs and toast and coffee, she went unerringly to the bare table at the window, then rolled the table and tray to where I might, by turning onto my left elbow, reach everything. I suspect she thought she was serving Hazard. I devoured every morsel in sight: then without further ado (Hazard had excused himself) I flung off the covers and asked the blind old lady where I might find my clothes.

Believe me, I did not for one whole month venture near the Eshpeter Ranch. I did not ever again myself encounter the supernatural, for the next encounter was to be Hazard's, not mine. He must surely have missed our afternoon conversations; on my first visit after so long an absence he was however too feeble to see me, having experienced I was informed something of a relapse.

I would not have returned to the ranch a few days later had not Martha herself sent me to the confrontation: she, unwittingly, asked me to deliver a message to Marie.

It was early in August now; the heat and the flies in the rink beyond the Coulee Hill Livery were quite unbearable; it was time for Martha to send her Arabs to the open range. On the morning of 6 August she asked me to drive out and ask Marie if she, Martha, might pay a visit on the evening of that same day.

I should have been supremely happy that sunlit morning, for in serving Martha I would have an opportunity further to study Hazard. Yet I felt a certain unease. Hazard's whereabouts, as I say, had been to Martha a mystery for a few weeks. But she had long since ceased to expect him during the busy spring and early summer while he was presumably travelling his stallion from farm to farm. He never wrote (I have always rejected the argument, advanced by some, that he was very nearly illiterate): yet he had appeared each autumn for thirteen years. She was confident he would appear again.

Of course I was eager for her to see him. But I can say with equal confidence that Hazard did not want to be seen in his present disgraceful circumstances. I delayed my visit until quite late in the afternoon.

I found the two of them, Marie and Hazard, having tea together on the porch; neither of them made the slightest effort to conceal the intimacy of the situation. Perhaps this irritated me, for I burst out from my car window without so much as turning off the engine: 'Martha Proudfoot would like to visit you this evening if she may, Marie. About pasturing her mares—'

I took Marie's silence to be an affirmative reply, and without waiting to learn more of her response or intentions I took my foot off the clutch and was gone.

26

It was, by all accounts, a very busy late afternoon on the Eshpeter Ranch. Most of the details of the day I have gleaned from my talks with Old Lady Eshpeter; she was herself briefly—confined is the word, I believe—to this jolly institution, and together we had many a delightful chat.

Hazard, after my departure, went off in a great hurry towards the barns to see Poseidon; only to discover when he got to the proper stall that Poseidon was absent. He went running back to the house; only to find now that Marie too was not to be located. Flustered, he returned to the barns and entered another, supposing he might have searched in the wrong one. Hazard had indeed become that lax in his concern for Poseidon; he hardly remembered where the big blue stallion was or what he looked like.

In passing from one barn to the next however—he had been through them twice—he heard Poseidon neigh. He went immediately to the corral from which the sound had issued.

Hazard for a moment was about to rejoice. As he first peeked between two of the crooked poplar poles that made up the large corral he beheld Poseidon, his great neck curved forward, his ears back, in the act of mounting. But as the horse lunged forward under the guidance of one man, a second raised—I blush to report something so unnatural—an artificial vagina to the erect member.

Artificial insemination, as you must understand, is possible only with genuine semen. And of course it must be collected. The artificial vagina—and I have examined one since, holding it with trembling hands before me—is made up of an outer tube of heavy rubber with, inside it, another tube or lining, this one of very thin rubber. The space between must be filled with water that has been heated to a temperature of not less than 105° F. and not more than 115° F. The male can be quite insistent about the proper—not only temperature—but pressure and lubrication as well. A special lubricant is, of course, available commercially. At the far end from the opening of this device, a beaker is so placed as to catch without waste or contamination the ejaculated semen.

There remains the problem of arousing the stallion to an appropriate physical state. Early investigators (and the Japanese were pioneers) used a mare in heat to arouse the stallion, at the last moment intruding the scientific contraption between the

133

passionate stallion and the impatient mare. But the two hired men who laboured before Hazard's eyes, inspired no doubt by Marie's vivid imagination, had hit upon quite another remedy.

27

A frame which resembled a giant sawhorse had been set up in the corral. This was covered in turn with heavy horsehide to protect the rising stallion from injuring himself on sharp corners or splinters of wood.

Incidentally, bulls and some stallions, recent studies suggest, can become so addicted to this simple and yet remarkable dummy that they prefer it to what is popularly termed, the real thing. But this had not as yet happened to Poseidon: on striking his hoofs against the wood he reared back, flinging the man at his head to the ground.

Hazard reacted by leaping to the top of the corral fence. But just as he was about to tumble down inside he heard a whip crack. Looking about from his unlikely perch, he saw Marie raise and swing her blacksnake again: it cracked at Poseidon's ear and he fell obediently into stillness.

Old Lady Eshpeter, as I say, became a colleague of mine in my contemplation of mankind's various ambitions. She sat beside my tub on whatever was most convenient (she was permitted by the dear crochety doctors to be my guest because, as they put it, she would not be scandalized by my insistent nakedness). There she sat, so oddly out of connection with the modern world in her long black dress and her button shoes: and we had a lark of a time, chattering and giggling like a pair of schoolgirls.

It was she who recounted to me the details of what followed. She argued that Hazard recognized immediately the advantages of the scheme. Charming woman that she was, she was also devious in her petty way. 'He was always clever,' she told me, 'and yet so considerate. What a rare combination.'

'We have to judge him by his actions,' I insisted. 'On that occasion he turned and ran.'

The old woman claimed to have sensitive ears. 'I can't stand loud, boastful voices,' she said.

'And I can't stand cowards,' I let her know. 'He was scared stiff. He was fleeing.' I sometimes banged an open palm against the side of my tub to accentuate a point. 'You admit yourself that he ran to Marie's car, jumped in, and drove away.'

'Precisely,' Mrs Eshpeter replied. 'He was a man of utter genius. He saw in a flash that his one horse could service not a dozen mares in one week but a hundred in one day.'

'The whimpering coward heard the whip and saw the woman. On top of everything else, he was a superstitious frog.' I quite forgot myself and nearly stood up. 'The man was scared half out of his wits. He couldn't begin to endure half of what I endured in that house of yours. Three times I went back. But Hazard Lepage: just one little moment of fright and off he went, scampering into the grass. He was lower than a snake's vest buttons.'

'Hazard Lepage,' the old woman said, pressing two fingers into her eyes, 'must have been the handsomest man alive. Nothing but kind words. Yet there wasn't a thing in the world he feared.'

'He went running to the priest,' I said.

'Of course,' she replied. 'Because he wanted to marry my daughter.'

'You're out of your mind,' I shouted, for I did now and then lose my temper at the old hag.

'He loved my daughter,' she said. 'My daughter nursed him.'

'He loved no one,' I said. 'Not that man.'

'My daughter saved him.'

'*Who* saved him?' I said. '*Who* saved him? You tell me *who* saved him.'

'He knew my daughter could save him.'

'He was running so hard,' I reminded her, 'he almost killed Martha Proudfoot in his haste.'

And then we both collapsed into gales of laughter. For you see, by a nice combination of circumstance and error, Hazard drove out of the lane just as Martha was driving in. The sun was low enough to be a glare on his line of vision; he did not see her as they met. She did not see him for she was too busy swinging into the ditch to avoid the car that wobbled directly towards her down the one-track lane, threatening her with annihilation.

Hazard, once he was safely out on the main road, drove directly to the skating rink behind the Coulee Hill hotel and livery barn. It was suppertime, the town was quiet. The beer parlour, as usual, had closed for an hour. The afternoon train had come and gone, with its clang of empty cream cans and its rumble of beer barrels onto the dray. The evening bus was not due for another two hours.

Hazard wheeled the old car down the middle of the street, turned into a side alley that took him behind the hotel, and promptly ran over a garbage can. It was this last gesture that caught the attention of three or four local residents. Quickly he jumped out of the car and hurried to the skating rink fence.

The sky was red beyond the rink; while the sun had not yet set, clouds hung in a purple bank along the horizon. Hazard leaned against the sagging fence and stared across the baked and dusty ground of the enclosure, over the planks that constituted the far side of the rink to that distant rim of cloud and sky. The five Arab horses, after a while, ceased to regard him with curiosity and went about the business of eating and dreaming and resisting flies.

What painful thoughts went through Hazard's mind in the slow departure of the sun?

Did he perchance see in those Arab mares a horse that was perfect in its docility, in its size and long life? Perhaps, just as a drowning man will review his own history, there flashed before his eyes all the history of equine glory. Perhaps he thought of those great stallions that shaped England's history for two and a half centuries. Hardly a dandy or a politician or a beggar or a king did not owe much of his quintessence to those great studs, the Byerly Turk, the Darley Arabian, and especially to the greatest of them all, the Godolphin Arabian. Did he think of Hernando Cortez, in 1518, conquering all Mexico with a force of eighteen men on horseback, bringing in that glorious act the Arab horse to the New World? Or did he think instead of the Narragansett Pacer, that breed that flourished throughout puritanical and revolutionary America, only to become as extinct as the woolly mammoth?

Confronting such knowledge, Hazard must have recognized that all decisions had become his. What a pity, that when man comes finally to his test and choice, he is alone and secret. O how I could tell you . . .

Was he perhaps tempted to turn from the rink and enter the hotel, going directly to Martha to say he was ready to take employment with her successful father? If so, he would have been rudely disappointed, for Martha was still out at the Eshpeter Ranch; he would have found me, his rival, busily washing beer glasses and wiping tables and sweeping the floor. I was by that evening risen in the good graces of Uncle Timothy to a degree I was never again to know.

At any rate, there he hesitated, Hazard Lepage, a studhorse man on whom a breed of greatness depended. Of that juncture of possibilities what can we honestly say? Only this: that Hazard stood for one hour hardly moving except to put one foot up on a board, then lowering that foot, kicking a thistle or pigweed (witnesses differed) in the process, and raising the other—

He might well have thought briefly of the nearly extinct Przewalski horse. Is not the Przewalski horse the horse that was pictured by a Stone Age artist in the caves of Lascaux some fifteen thousand years ago? It must then have ranged wild over all of Europe; in recent years only a herd of one stallion and seven mares has been sighted by man, in the Gobi Desert of Outer Mongolia. But I drift into mere speculation—

Hazard urinated briefly, both feet on the earth, taking some care to knock the seeds from a thistle (witnesses agreed), appearing all the while to contemplate; then, even as he closed his fly, he turned from the object of his contemplation.

F   137

28

You who stare blankly in your musty basement flats, in your rented upstairs apartments, in your so-called 'living' rooms full of TV and offspring, in your king-sized beds; you hot-pants secretaries skulking behind your typewriters, you matrons sweating in the illusory stink of the beauty parlour (forgive me if I smile), you executives hunched bony-kneed and hairy and straining in the john, you schoolboys in the library, using my precious wisdom to conceal your furtive lusting after the girl who doesn't know her skirt is up and her legs spread (or at least she lets you think she doesn't know); all you who think you do not live in a madhouse—do not smirk at Hazard's inability to recognize and to do what was best.

If ever I complete this magnificent study of that lonely man I shall call it not simply HAZARD LEPAGE, THE BIOGRAPHY OF A MODERN MARTYR, HIS MORTAL LIFE AND IMMORTAL ACCOMPLISHMENTS, but rather, by devious means pointing to more significant dimensions, THE STINTING OF MARTHA PROUDFOOT.

But once again, dear reader, I find myself in a corner. Art would find a neat way out; life is not so obliging. While I located at least three witnesses to Hazard's vigil at the skating rink, I will never, as you shall well understand, learn *exactly* what happened during the next two hours.

This much is certain. Hazard went to see the priest; the old priest was not home. Mrs Laporte, his housekeeper, answered the door. She had been playing solitaire and still held half the deck in her left hand, the five of hearts showing as the bottom card.

Out of courtesy she asked Hazard to come in and sit down and have a cup of tea, for not only did she recognize him, but he was famous in the parish for not having attended Mass in twenty-four years. Perhaps Mrs Laporte had visions of winning a soul back to God. At any rate Hazard, in his extreme anxiety, in his state of unmitigated agitation, said in reply, 'Sit down be diddled. I've got to lie down or fall down. My backside is killing me.'

Mrs Laporte herself, at fifty-one, was the picture of good health. She, however, seemed to be the last person to recognize this; during the previous two years she had talked day and night to anyone who would listen of nothing but her hot flashes and her failing memory, her ungrateful daughters, her no-good boozer of a husband who neglected her by staying up North and who beat her and robbed her when he came to visit, her inability to sleep at night, her dizzy spells, her sweating until the bed-sheets were wringing wet— But it must be added also, tribulation had made her extremely pious.

Hazard, of course, knew nothing of what I have just mentioned. He saw before him a woman dressed in a severe brown dress, her hair tinted a silvery-gray; her full white apron might have belonged to a nurse. 'You've come to the right place,' she said to Hazard. 'Between me and the father and his dog—' she indicated an old black setter asleep on the only couch in the room— 'we have just about every ache going. But you've added something new.'

'I'm a walking pain in the arse,' Hazard said, by way of apology.

The kind lady closed the front door and took him by the arm. 'I just last week cleaned the spare bedroom. Can you make it up these stairs ?'

29

I too would like the preceding chapter to be more explicit. But what can I add that is both relevant and accurate ? She had varicose veins ? Her breasts were losing their jostle and bounce ?

No, relevancies are those very things which one might at first glance dismiss. I, for instance, have developed remarkably tough calluses on my own behind. I mentioned this in passing to Old Lady Eshpeter. I had persuaded her as a little joke to sit in my tub while I perched on the rim; she was 'taking a turn at the wheel'. 'Demeter,' she responded to my gossipy comment, 'to break a spell cast by a spirit you must say three times, "*Lech mich am Arsch*."'

She said as much to the poor devil of a priest every time he knocked at her door. I tried it on my doctors; they threatened to throw me out of the place if I didn't learn to behave.

30

Perhaps Hazard intended only to rest until the good father returned from whatever mission of mercy occupied him at that hour. The old priest walked with a cane and was not likely to accomplish anything in a hurry. Hazard must have found the company of Mrs Laporte relaxing after the tumult of his previous relationship.

Staring at Martha Proudfoot's five virgin mares for an hour, he surely recognized that his first duty was to recover Poseidon from the clutches of Marie Eshpeter. And he may well have known that Father Lockner for years had been seeking an excuse to exorcise the spirits from that notorious ranch; on one occasion he had taken the liberty of delivering a bottle of holy water to Mrs Eshpeter. Within minutes a large piece of plaster fell from the kitchen ceiling (he was having a small glass of rye) and broke his great toe.

Hazard went to the proper source for help; it was a factor quite beyond his control that only the housekeeper should be there to greet him at the door. Empires have collapsed for lesser reasons.

All I assert with confidence is this: it was the priest himself who first noticed the flames coming out of an upstairs window of the fine priest's house there beside his church. He ran to a small red box inside the church door and broke the appropriate pain of glass with the appropriate iron bar. Far away, a siren wailed. In four minutes the town's only fire truck was on the scene, along with half the residents of Coulee Hill. The house, obviously, was doomed to burn down to its foundations; the problem was to save the church, and the firemen set to work with commendable skill.

In all modesty I must now intrude my own activities into this extremely objective account of the life of one good man.

The flames ate the siding off the upper story of the big wooden house; the 2 × 4s stood for a moment pencilled against the hunger of the fire, then they themselves dissolved into black smoke (more from tarpaper than from wood)—and nothing. It was just as a corner of the roof exploded beautifully and brilliantly against the darkening sky that I heard a scream.

For some reason, I alone heard it. I had left the hotel immediately I heard the siren (it was only three doors down from the hotel); Uncle Timothy, swearing roundly in my direction, had dragged himself away from the comfortable desk in the lobby to provide for the dozen or so customers who by that time inhabited the beer parlour. It was as if I had been given a call to battle.

As I say, I alone heard the scream, and only with some difficulty did I persuade anyone that a scream had in fact been given. Fortunately, a town gossip there in our midst suddenly remarked that Mrs Laporte was not in the watching crowd: and promptly gave a scream of her own. Four very brave high school boys as if at a command raced towards the front door of the house.

They were greeted, on opening the door, by no little smoke, though the fire for the moment was concentrated mostly at the top of the building and towards the rear. When the four boys disappeared inside and did not for quite some time reappear, a hush of expectation fell over the watching crowd. It was then I went forward myself.

Imagine stepping into a burning building in time to see a single bed (minus its mattress) come plummeting through the ceiling and onto the living room carpet. The mind hesitates to accept the evidence of its own senses. But in avoiding the consequent shower of sparks I ran directly into the embrace of what later proved to be Mrs Laporte. She was crying aloud and repeatedly in her anguish: 'He's dead he's dead he's dead he's dead.'

I had the presence of mind to free myself from the faceful of bosom that proved more suffocating than the smoke. Like someone gone to save a drowning man, I was myself in danger of being drowned by that person's panic. I struggled, and only by resorting to something resembling violence did I free myself so I might act. Mrs Laporte clung to me sobbing. I carried her out of the burning house, into the fresh air.

I thought for a moment the applause and the cries of relief were for me. In fact I was preceded by the four young men, each of them carrying one corner of a mattress. Mrs Laporte now struggled as determinedly to be free of my arms as she had earlier struggled to hold me tight. She ran to catch up with the mattress.

The applause died. Then I too saw why the mattress was being carried as if its burden must be as precious as life. Consider my utter astonishment, my shudder of dread and concern, when I saw on the mattress a motionless, naked figure, and on the figure a full beard.

Mrs Laporte followed after the four young men, continuing to cry out the expression with which she had earlier assaulted my ears ('He's dead'). She was given someone's jacket to wear over her dress and apron.

I ripped off my white beerslinger's jacket and flung it as best I might over Hazard's private parts. Someone had found a blanket and now covered him from head to toe. Two women were trying to restrain Mrs Laporte. The four young men (pall-bearers, one is tempted to write), having behaved so bravely, were at a loss for what to do next. Again I took the initiative: I led them to where they might slide their burden into the back of a small van from which had just been unloaded additional buckets and ladders.

Mrs Laporte persisted in crying out her hysterical proclamation. In the midst of the embarrassment and pain that we all felt, I suggested to the owner of the van that the limp and motionless figure be delivered immediately to the hotel.

31

At that time in Coulee Hill the only refrigerated space of any consequence was the icehouse attached to the Coulee Hill beer parlour. Buried deep in the great mounds of fresh sawdust were enough rectangular blocks of blue-white ice to chill the infinite kegs of beer through all the hot summer. The dark old room itself stayed cool because of the ice so near the surface of the sawdust; on more than one occasion a body had there awaited the arrival of the undertaker, who must be telephoned and who must then travel something like seventy solitary miles.

A group of men came to the door as the van approached the hotel. They saw the covered figure and took off their caps; without speaking they obeyed my signals and together we made a quiet procession of it, winding our way among the beer tables. Head bowed, I led onward, pushing chairs aside, picking up one or two empties that might be knocked over. The few customers who had not come to the door sat now with their caps in their hands, not touching their full glasses. We went past the cash register and the rinse tubs and out through the back door.

The icehouse had a kind of appeal all its own; on a scorching hot day it was not difficult to imagine the comfort and ease of stretching out there for three or four hours, waiting for the hearse to come skidding around the corner and out of the heat and dust of Highway 313. Hazard, under his blanket, on his mattress, was lowered gently on to the soft banks of sawdust. I inhaled deeply the cool odour of sawn spruce and pine. Then I swung the thick door to and the dark room closed on its scar of resounding stillness.

Martha was not yet home from the Eshpeters when my loyal band of helpers re-entered the beer parlour to quaff a glass or two of consolation and refreshment. God knows, a beer in that cosy place is as much a part of the ritual of death in Coulee Hill as is the digging of the grave. But mundane details would have to wait, I decided. The priest was quite busy enough. I bought a round for the house. Within five minutes two men arrived from the scene of the fire, bearing the assuring news that the church itself was past all danger and sure to be saved.

32

On that historic night I managed finally, in spite of my emotional upset and concern, to telephone Notikeewin and the undertaker: Lt John Backstrom was only recently back from overseas and eager once again to resume his profession. I returned from the telephone in the hotel lobby to the beer parlour resolved somehow to carry on and do the work my uncle expected of me. To make matters worse, I found a number of people speculating about the cause and implications of the recent tragedy: and, I confess with embarrassment, even joking about it. I anticipated Martha's return momentarily; to make my wait endurable at all (I feared for her even more than for myself) I was compelled to listen to the jokesters.

'This undertaker,' a farmer from St Leo was saying, 'he was preparing a body when he noticed the fellow had the biggest whang he had ever laid eyes on. He called in a friend who was just then doing a little work in the next room. "Look at this," he says to his friend. "Did you ever see one like this?" "I've got one just like it," the friend says. "The hell you have, that big?" the undertaker says. "No," the friend says. "That dead." '

The laughter was enormous; it rattled and smashed at my eardrums. Only the obligation to go on wiping tables and emptying ashtrays kept me from passing out. 'I'll bet Mrs Laporte could have raised it,' someone added: and got a few more lascivious laughs.

The speculation then began as to how Hazard came to be naked, and I can assure you the uninformed guesses were not in accord with my own estimate of Mrs Laporte. On my first annual vacation (I never stay the full three weeks) outside my present domicile I went immediately to interview the poor woman. Why

I did not do so at the time will shortly become apparent. But when I called upon her, finally, in the new ranch-style priest's house with its picture window for all the world to look in at, she wanted to speak only of Hazard's sincerity. 'He was a sincere man,' she told me over her teacup, 'his heart was in the right place.' I tried to fish out of her something more explicit. 'He meant everything he said,' she told me, not giving a clue as to what he had in fact said. 'It's not as if I was single,' she added. We ate, between us, a box of chocolate mints. We discussed her numerous ailments. But not until I was leaving did she herself ask a question. She caught my hand as I was turning to depart, and looked deeply into my eyes. 'He needed a little money. Did you by any chance find the twenty dollars—'

In the beer parlour, of course, Hazard was turning out quite a rapscallion. The general opinion had it that more than a few women would grieve at the sad news. 'The communion rail,' one perennial customer (Mr Nelson, long an admirer of Martha) ventured, 'will be crowded Sunday morning.' Another (Mr Bessai, also an admirer) told the wicked little story about the famous butcher and the wife who was never satisfied. The laughter had commenced even before he concluded: 'Shultz is dead.'

I slipped away for a moment to peek into the icehouse, unable in the face of such talk to believe what had happened. Outside the hotel the night was uncommonly still; the riddle of the stars rained its blessing on our unbelieving heads. I hardly opened the squeaking door on the silence in the icehouse before I turned and fled back into the company of those roisterers I had just forsaken.

'Didn't get up and walk away, did he?' someone asked.

Unable to speak, I shook my head. I couldn't bear it. Martha must arrive soon or I would collapse into tears; I went to the front door of the beer parlour and looked up and down the street as if my very pain must bring her home.

Again, the silence. The cars were parked in neat and silent rows; the street lamps shone with unblinking dumb insistence, each a galaxy of moths and flies. Across the street two gas pumps bled their pale yellow light on to the oil-stained gravel. Beyond an unused water pump the squat railway station was the indifferent red of dried blood. The grain elevators stood tall in a row against the farthest darkness, their eyeless heads unbowed.

I stepped outside, for my mind was beginning to wander: I let myself think too much of Martha's coming grief, her future destroyed and gone. What would she do in her loneliness? The crazy thought came to my mind that I must go tell her Arab mares: but just as I let the screen door close behind me I saw a car turn from the main road onto the street. I knew that car so well that even its headlights were familiar.

I stepped back into the beer parlour; I raced through a swinging door into the lobby of the hotel; I went to the desk where Uncle Tim sat working on last month's accounts. 'Uncle Tim,' I said. 'Uncle Timothy.'

I feared that he had not yet forgiven my earlier neglect of my obligations. Little did I realize that in the hour preceding that moment I had come to recognize the futility of all labour and would not thereafter labour again. Wisdom comes strangely to our reluctant minds.

'Yes?' my uncle inquired.

'She's here.' My fingers rattled on the counter against which I now leaned.

'Well?' he continued.

I managed to shake my head. 'I can't—break the news.'

Uncle Timothy closed the ledger and with a quick motion managed to get to his feet. I swear the wicked man wore a smile of relief, even of pleasure.

33

The biographer is a person afflicted with sanity. He is a man who must first of all be sound of mind, and in the clarity of his own vision he must ride out the dark night, ride on while all about him falls into chaos. The man of the cold eye and the steady hand, he faces for all of humanity the ravishments and the terrors of existence.

Compassion took me at the closing hour (10.30 pm) from the hotel to the icehouse. Martha had been absent for a total of thirty-six minutes since her father spoke his abrupt eulogy; momentarily I had expected her to come to me to state her wishes.

Supposing at last that she could not bring herself to approach me, I went to her; timidly I knocked at the icehouse walls. But I did not wait to be invited in; I could not expect Martha in the presence of—Hazard—to speak. I opened the door.

What follows is the end.

Hazard, let me recapitulate, beneath the blanket, beneath the coat I had so lovingly laid upon his torso, was stark naked. Martha, in her disbelief that her beloved must be dead, put first a hand upon his bare foot (one thinks of the death of Socrates). It was, apparently, warmer than she had anticipated, though nevertheless fearfully cold in that room full of sawdust and buried ice. Thus did she in succession put her hand upon his ankle bone, his shinbone, and his knee.

The groping hand was to grope on, for what she would ignore in life, Martha could not ignore in death. Old Blue was next in line in that sequence. So regal and so tall and brave there in the long twilight, she touched first a finger to the cold nose of the mystery, then a second finger to the shrivelled fact, then a comforting hand. Superstition would have it that in death there is one final standing to and Martha, at this stirring, grieved all the more.

Even as I now call him back with my pencil and paper did she, perhaps, hoping she might massage life back into death itself, with the long pale fingers of her right hand ever so gently administer there in the near darkness beneath my white jacket a kind of last feverish call?

34

What a moment of astonishment she must have known, mastering that sturdy pillar of the night. I should write an address to intending censors: you judges in skirts that conceal your mortal manhood, read slowly, and then but gently give rebuke to those who would emulate your privilege. Martha was champion against our promised end. Death was a nightmare presence bent on snuffing Hazard into a longer darkness; it was the crone and succubus, the ancient fiend turned female that in the night of dream has fatal intercourse with men. Yes, and the moon was a cold bright disc on the sky: Mare Frigoris, Mare Hiemis, Mare Incognito. But Martha strove against those seas of dust like Herakles against the hate of Diomedes and his man-eating mares. Martha was all curiosity to understand, to feel: and the mystery took form in her hand, became unshrivelled and yet more the mystery, at once silk smooth and iron hard, boneless becoming bone of blood. There was no tree of knowledge to equal that one in her will to know, no ladder and no hill. *Axis mundi*, the wise men tell us, and on it the world turns.

35

The dead man opened his eyes to the grip of four fingers and a thumb, to a quick impatience that might erase the hanging gloom. Martha believed him dead; the dead man said, 'Hurry.'

36

In the chill hush of that August night she was all love and pity and concern, warming his naked body with her hands and kisses.

On that death's mattress, she, flinging off her clothes against the sawdust and the ice, took home her hero's body to her body's joy. Hazard could not so much as turn upon his side, for exhaustion and cold, but Martha rode to her new glory until the night must have burned for shame at her abandon. It is only travelling takes us home. The bending sun. The Lucifer night. What colour were her eyes? I cannot remember. As blue as ice, I would wish. There in that dumb doorway she stood to tell me, her honeyed hair a river down her back, the sawdust on her cheeks; there she stood so barely decent in the only dark that clothed her body; shameless there in the dark that was not black enough for her (I saw the jasper glint of her wet and swollen nipples) laughing and crying she came to close the door against my face; and then, all modesty gone, 'Old Blue,' she cried, 'Old Blue,' she was laughing.

Young Poseidon came to my mind: deserted, forsaken, neglected beyond all hope of love in his state of abject possession. It was decreed there that I, in the final analysis, through my devotion and concern, should save the Lepage horse from extinction.

37

I too was young that night. At the stroke of twelve on that night of Martha's debauchery, I drove four mares from the skating rink beyond the livery barn and the icehouse. I fitted a bridle to the mouth of the fifth mare. Trembling at my own ignorance (and Martha had never let me ride), I climbed to the fifth mare's back. My journey had begun. Hazard had failed.

Was it not I who remarked, every journey is a journey home? Our departure was not marred by the barking of a single stray mongrel or bitch. We stayed to the roadside, the dead grass and stinkweed of a dry August muffling the fall of hoofs. I did not drive but rather led my harem of mares. And I felt not the slightest pang of guilt: history tells of a conquering army that one day took for tribute a herd of twenty thousand Arab horses, each of them snow white.

Riding in the hush of darkness, I discovered dawn. The birds came chirping alive: the meadowlark, the blackbird. Two crows called from the horizon. A hawk on the crossbar of a telephone pole unfolded its broad wings to the promise of sun. A deer, its antlers sharp and upright, would not shy from my presence and watched my caravan go by. A porcupine slid reluctantly from our dusty way, its path like a ship's wake on the bending grass.

The dawn was prairie pale, and I was not frightened of its wide emptiness. I had the courage to stop my procession on the road; alone I walked into the lane and then to the yard of the Eshpeter Ranch. Alone I freed Poseidon from his captors.

That morning I was D. Proudfoot, Studhorse Man. We continued west and south: on my mare I led the stallion. The other mares followed. I let them all graze for an hour, in a wild meadow where they might taste bergamot and daisies with their grass; I let them drink from a drying slough, splashing their long heads into the water, their bellies visibly swelling full. A muskrat made an arrow of its nose, then dived and did not ever rise where I might see him. Ten ducklings, too downy to fly, were scolded into the cattails.

And I was happy then. And I might have been happy. The sun was hot on my eyes. Approaching the river hills we found where a man had cut down the poplars into heaps and then left them. The horses waded to their thighs in roses. I ate red raspberries off a bush. Without so much as dismounting I milked the choke-cherries off a branch and into my mouth. And I wondered if I had always been happy.

It was the hottest part of the afternoon when we arrived at the valley's edge, at the ancient buffalo jump overlooking Wildfire Lake. Quickly we found the mansion. And it was as Hazard had told me: so splendid and unlikely that I might have come to a dream. Alone it rode on the precipice, the untouched grass around it waving in a small wind. We were weary and we rested, the horses and I.

And yet I was not dreaming. The horses lounged into the shade on the east side of the mansion. I found the gangplank covering the front steps; the door was not locked. Hazard had never bothered to take the boards off most of the downstairs windows. I might have stayed outside: I did not lift the knocker but went in to where three shotguns leaned in a row against a bookshelf weighted with boxes of shells.

The rooms were as Hazard had left them. The bay windows opened out of the dining room: on the manure outside the pigweeds and goldenrod had found time to grow. The parlour with its patterned walls, its lions and its fleurs-de-lis, smelled cool, smelled richly of horses. On the bookcase behind the guns were three mousetraps in a matchbox, copper rivets and ivory rings, a schoolboy's ruler, a throng of medicines.

Eugene Utter had stayed only in the library. A horse blanket lay in a heap on the leather couch where he had slept. The roll-top desk was covered with crumbs and empty tin cans. In the boredom of his long and futile wait he had tried to read, apparently, for the first volume of *The General Stud Book* was open, not at a mare's history, but to the 'Obituary of Stallions'. I quote now from memory: 'HARTLEY'S BLIND HORSE, in 1742 . . . PARTNER, the latter end of the year 1747 . . . CRAB, on Christmas Day 1750 . . . THE GODOLPHIN ARABIAN, in December 1753, age uncertain but supposed 28 . . . BLAZE, in 1756 . . . WHYNOT, in 1764 . . . REGULUS . . . LITTLE DRIVER . . . SNAP . . . PHOENOMENON, soon after landing in America, 1798 . . . WOODPECKER . . . KING FERGUS . . . CROP, late in the year 1801 . . . PRECIPITATE, before landing in America, 1803 . . .'

I held the old book in my two hands that now were rubbed shiny by the reins I had held all day and smelled of leather and horse's sweat. My crotch ached pleasantly. I sat for a long time in the leather chair beside the roll-top desk, neglecting all the work I must do. Yet even as I loafed my purpose was becoming clearer and more clear.

38

You will recall that Louis David Riel, charged with treason for trying to save his nation from destruction, repudiated the plea of insanity that his defence council proposed. He was hanged on 16 November 1885. I too was shortly to be branded with that unlikely tag, legally insane; and how unjustly, you shall presently see.

As afternoon turned to evening there in Hazard's mansion, I found the will to perform at least a few of my essential duties (one must ask finally if *any* form of activity is truly a pleasure). I pumped water from the cistern and watered my six horses in a wooden tub outside the kitchen: Hazard had taken down a length of eaves trough and fixed it so that one might fill the tub easily from the old iron pump on the kitchen sink. The pantry proved to contain two sacks of oats. I carried out a pailful (after adding just a smidgen of Spanish fly) and I fed to each mare a heap of kernels on the ground. I carried out a double ration to my Poseidon; he too must prepare for his new responsibilities.

I set a woodfire to burning in the kitchen stove. I found some powdered milk of the kind that was popular during the war: a mouse had nibbled its way into the container but had done no great damage. I found both salt and sugar for my porridge, and a lovely china pot in which to make tea.

The valley below the mansion was endlessly still and completely devoid of human life. I sat and ate on the lower front veranda where I might watch the quiet valley and its long lake. A hawk soared in the empty sky above me, vanishing and reappearing and vanishing again as I strained my eyes to follow its fortunes. Near at hand, a gopher after a while ventured brazenly out of its hole to study this new intruder. My horses, their meal done, galloped together across the prairie towards a grove of poplar. Freed of the few flies that tormented them, they came back to me and were docile.

I had found my peace; I saw what I must do to keep it. Washing my few simple dishes, setting each in its appointed place in the cupboards, I now proceeded to load the three shotguns. Carefully I fashioned a cartridge belt of an old piece of harness, and I wore a band of extra shotgun shells across my chest. Now for the first time I ventured upstairs, carrying my arsenal.

Hazard himself claimed he only slept in seven different beds to avoid the chore of making beds each day. He liked a clean and well-made bed; he hated making them. Painted in crude gilt letters on the headboard of each of six beds was the name of a stallion (the first was illegible). Five of the beds, as I may have remarked earlier, were messed up. The sixth, without sheets or a pillow, bore the name: POSEIDON. The seventh bed, neatly made up, bore on its high headboard only the initial 'D' and a space for a name. I chose that bed as my own.

Fortunately it was in a corner room, with one window looking to the east, a second and larger window looking to the north and facing onto the hardly discernible prairie trail that approached the mansion. I left one shotgun by the bed.

Next I went to the bedroom that was diagonally across the upstairs (though in fact down a long L-shaped corridor) from my room. There two windows faced south and west. I saw that the steep bank of the river valley would discourage invaders from using that approach. Yet I left a gun in the corner of the room between the two windows.

Each of the three guns was double-barrelled. By carrying one gun with me and having auxiliaries available, I could fire off four quick shots in any one direction, and in the ensuing confusion I would have time to reload before the enemy resumed his attack.

Further, to my advantage, the north wall was not encumbered by the two-level veranda that ran around the other three sides: an enemy approaching directly down the trail would have to contemplate an assault on a smooth and vertical surface.

The sun had gone down to where it must shine more brightly as a reflection in my windows than on the horizon. Taking a pailful of oats to lure the mares (it proved unnecessary) I now went outside and called to Poseidon. He came at once to my hand, massive and calm. I led him up the gangplank and in at the front door. The mares, obediently, even eagerly, followed: Martha had taught me the proper care of horses. It was quite dark by the time I finished currying and combing the six quiet animals.

And yet they were no longer so quiet. Two of the mares, it seemed to me, had begun to vie for Poseidon's attention. The ceilings of the dining room and parlour, I gauged, were quite high enough so as not to interfere with Poseidon's pleasure. Carefully I locked all the windows and bolted the only door. With a final word of blessing I left my beloved creatures to their own devices and I slipped upstairs to commence my vigil.

O that Martha had been there to listen to the night: not to the appalling monotony of the insects outside my many windows, not to the coyotes in the valley: but to the horses in the rooms below me. The night was long and memorable beneath a blaze of moon. Poseidon and his harem of Arab mares had only my occasional fond gaze to interrupt their dallyings; the victory was sweet for all; love clattered in that splendid night.

It was at the crack of dawn that Poseidon most pleasured himself, as is the fashion, I am told, of wild stallions on the open prairies. At the same time, going my rounds from room to room and bed to bed, carrying my loaded and cocked shotgun as if I must defy the four winds themselves, I must have somehow fallen asleep. I was awakened by what sounded like an engine.

I was awakened by what I thought was an automobile churring its way across the prairie like a vicious insect. I opened my eyes against the slant of sun. All was quiet. My horses made no sound below me. I was flat on my back on my bed, my shotgun lay between my legs, my arms cradling the warm blue barrel to my cheek. I thought I had dreamed.

My clothes stuck to my flesh when I sat up, and I tugged them free. Again I listened; hearing nothing I went to the window facing north. The prairie was mottled with clumps of poplar, their leaves shimmering in a slight breeze. I saw it must be mid-morning; it was time I watered and fed my spent horses. I might have gone to do so (and thus been taken by surprise) had not the sun just then glinted on a chrome bumper.

The car moved slowly from behind a grove; the driver, obviously, was new to his task. Patience, I told myself. Patience. I must be patient. I lifted the gun to the open window, sighted down the long barrel. It's only a shotgun, I told myself. Be infinitely patient.

The car began to swing in an arc. The driver presumed to come into my very yard. He began to slow. Aiming to have the buckshot whiz across the front of the gleaming white hood, I gave the trigger a delicate squeeze.

Not having allowed for the forward motion of the automobile (it was, by the way, Uncle Timothy's favourite), I happened to put quite a dent in the hood. I could not help but laugh at the frantic response; the car swung like a turpentined dog and fled to a nearby stand of poplar.

It was Hazard who came trotting out of the trees a few minutes later.

'Halloo!' he called.

I broke the gun and, waiting for him to come closer, I took out the spent shell, sniffed its delicious dark orifice, and worked a loaded shell free from the belt I wore across my chest. Hazard called again.

'Traitor,' I shouted back. 'You have betrayed your own cause.'

'Demeter?' Hazard called. 'Demeter? Is that you?'

'No,' I shouted back, mocking him. 'No. I am the man who breeds horses. Who are you?'

'I'm your friend.' He took a step. 'I'm with you.'

'Stop,' I shouted. 'Stay, friend.'

He cupped his hands against his beard. 'Martha is worried about you.'

What could I say?

I pulled both triggers at once. What else could I do to silence him? I had not quite prepared myself for what was to happen: the kick of the gun, the discharge, knocked me flat on the bed. But I scrambled up through the sudden sweet smell of gunpowder and in a moment had the gun loaded again. I switched to the second twelve-gauge and its cold barrels. I returned to the window.

I had missed the little bastard; but he didn't have enough sense to turn and vanish. Instead, retreating a few steps, he yelled something towards the poplar grove; and I saw Martha coming to join him.

'Go back to your icehouse,' I shouted. 'Go back to your sawdust man.'

Apparently she could not hear me; she walked a few steps closer, carrying something in her two hands.

'Demeter,' she called. 'Dear dear Demeter, don't you love your own flesh—'

'I'll shoot,' I yelled. I closed my left eye and with the right I fastened the front sight of the twin barrels on Martha's pussy.

'Demeter,' Martha called. 'I've brought you a lunch. I've brought you something to eat.'

It was that way in the hotel; she was always heaping food onto my plate, making me an extra sandwich. 'Set it down and go away,' I called.

'I must talk to you,' she insisted.

'Go away.'

'But aren't you hungry?' she called.

Finally I asked that she approach the house alone and that Hazard return to the car. Hazard, after some disagreement, yielded to the arrangement. When he disappeared behind the distant bush I raced downstairs and unbarred the front door. Martha entered the house and I barred the door again and led her to the library and the roll-top desk. She opened the basket.

The odour of freshly baked biscuits came up from the unfolded towel. And then I saw there were two cups, two plates, two napkins, two knives, two spoons . . .

'You made this for me?' I asked.

She hesitated. And then she answered: 'Yes.'

Martha had told me a lie. I don't like lying of any sort. I went to the door of the room; I went outside and slammed the door and locked it tight.

'Demeter?' Martha called from the darkness—for you see the windows of the library were carefully boarded shut. She tapped softly on the door. 'D?'

'Yes, Martha,' I replied.

'Demeter, what are you doing?'

I went upstairs and out onto the veranda in time to catch Hazard approaching the front door.

'Stand still,' I ordered.

Hazard looked up at the barrels of the shotgun and stood still. 'Where's Martha?' he asked.

'Martha,' I said, 'is staying with me.'

'I'll smash the door down,' Hazard said.

'I'll shoot you,' I said.

'No,' Hazard said. 'You wouldn't.' And he had the gall to smile.

My arms for a moment went limp, and I almost dropped the gun I held pointed at his skull. I wanted to cry; just for a moment I wanted to cry at the sadness of it all. But then, by the electrifying charge of my own inspiration, I was saved. 'It'll take you five minutes to break into this house.' I waited, smiling now in my turn. 'And while you're breaking in *I'll go downstairs and shoot your stallion.*'

I swear that Hazard blanched right through his thicket of beard. He tried to speak and his voice failed. He took a step, I could not tell whether forward or backward.

'You come one step closer,' I said, 'and I'll scatter that stallion's brains all over the ceiling. I'll blow it into a heap of bones.'

'Martha—'

'Martha is fine. She and I are planning to have lunch,' I explained. 'I want you to leave now. And if I see you around here before tomorrow morning, I'm going to hold this shotgun up between Poseidon's eyes and pull both triggers. I'll fasten his tail to a pole and fly it from the veranda. And I mean what I say, Mr Lepage.'

Hazard looked up again at the twin barrels of my gun. Then he turned and walked away. And I myself did not move until I saw the car turn and leave, raising behind it a tail of gray and powdery dust.

39

Martha played something of a joke on me; she somehow hooked and braced the door of the library from inside, so that I was unable to enter. It was a turn of events I hadn't anticipated.

And yet my second evening was, if possible, a greater pleasure than the first. Now my energy was boundless, my confidence supreme. I openly exercised my six horses in the fields around my mansion. I was able to pick an empty syrup pail full of saskatoons in the grove where Hazard claimed to have found an Indian's grave (I found nothing). I sat in a rocking chair on the high veranda, looking down into the valley, watching the drift of shadow and darkness into the spruce-crowded ravines and the gray, eroded coulees, watching the narrow lake turn from a burnished gold to the most extravagant lavender.

I pitched manure through the open bay window; I ate my porridge and drank my tea; I read for half an hour at the kitchen table. Noticing a bleached skull in the tall grass not far from the front door, I fired two practice shots, neatly splitting the old bone with my second try. Then I set about further barricading and nailing up windows in preparation for what I anticipated would be a considerable siege: for half the men in Coulee Hill, I guessed, would shortly come like so many ardent suitors to cry out their pleas. I made certain that Martha could not open the door that she would not open to me: and I went upstairs to another night's rest and vigil.

Dawn found me in the prime of condition. The first daylight I spent in grooming my horses and in brushing what threatened to become a full beard. My horses took the sun for a while (I picked two bouquets of wild sunflowers for their rooms), then all of us retreated behind our barred door.

Martha did not answer to any of my calls, but I heard her stirring about in her self-created little prison.

At something like 9 am a column of three cars approached across the prairie towards my mansion; a dozen nincompoops had ignored Hazard's request that I be left to his devices and were resolved that I must be, like some strange wild animal, captured alive. I must add with considerable pleasure that their resolve did not long persist in the face of an exuberance of buckshot.

I had worked out a scheme whereby I might empty all six barrels of my three shotguns in rather short order. The first wave of attackers called it a morning before the sun was decently up in the sky.

By 11 o'clock a total of eighteen cars and wagons were parked in stalemate beyond the range of my weaponry; the numerous spectators (including a number of beer-parlour hangabouts) had brought along sandwiches and cases of refreshments. And a rousing time they had of it, I don't mind telling you.

Three young lads took to playing a game of 'I can get closer than you' for their girl friends. I let them come well within range, then peppered the cockiest one in the arse. His beloved had a gay time of it, trying her Red Cross bandages on that wound.

Four grown men, inebriated no doubt, tried to approach my stronghold in a heavy tank wagon; I shot a horse dead in its tracks and the four scoundrels had occasion to sober up, for they took cover in the wagon until still another fool on a bicycle distracted me on the west side of the house. I missed him by inches; but I did have the satisfaction of hearing him holler and scream when in his panic he rode his bicycle over the cliff. Located as I was I could hear much of what was said, including Hazard's eloquent (I smile) entreaties to all that I be shown some respect.

Then an RCMP constable came driving up in his pretentious automobile; all decked out in his yellow stripes he came mincing and prancing up and commanded me to do something or other in the name of the law, indicating to me at the same time that he carried no gun. I gave the rascal a shoeshine that he'll never forget—if he stopped running long enough to admire it.

I could easily, I recognized, hold out forever; except that I might in time run out of ammunition. Anticipating that the enemy had in turn anticipated this eventuality, I planned, when my last shell was spent, to retreat into the cellar. I had placed in the darkness down there beside the dry well a short length of rope with which I might secure Martha and two butcher knives and a pitchfork, intending to make my last stand in hand-to-hand combat.

I saw a man in black emerge from a distant car and expected I must now endure the platitudes of heaven, the rosy promise of salvation in exchange for my earthly surrender. I was preparing a prayer such as that eager martyr had never heard, when I recognized him to be not a trader in souls but rather the limping figure of my Uncle Tad.

He came marching, bobbing along on his cane, straight at me. I waited, resolved that I would not fire until I could quite literally see the whites of his eyes. But he stopped just as he was coming into range. 'Okay, okay, take it easy, boy,' he puffed now, brandishing his cane. He was as big as a barn door. 'We want to help you, boy.'

'You could help by holding your picnic somewhere else,' I replied.

'We want to smoke a peace pipe,' he called.

'I can't hear you,' I called back. I stayed just out of sight inside my bedroom window. The glare of the hot sun beyond the cool room dazzled my eyes, and I had to keep them in perfect focus. Uncle Tad stirred without thinking, pulled his big cane from the earth and started forward again.

'Wait,' I shouted.

'Wait, nothing,' he said. 'We're going to make you a bargain.'

'Stop!' I shouted. I gave the fool a fair chance. 'STOP.'

Those horses,' he called. 'We'll trade you the mares—'

I gave a delicious squeeze to the trigger.

I had hoped to get Uncle Tad right square in the skull; instead I nicked him in the balls (and might have done better had not his cane been in the way).

The scoundrel rolled and screamed in the dusty grass: 'Get that crazy bastard!' was the last coherent thing I heard the unfortunate fellow say. It was, as you see, to be his word against mine; he had a small fortune behind him.

But to be pronounced insane, one must demonstrably *not* know the nature and quality of one's act. I knew with immodest clarity that by my heroism and concern the Lepage horse must be given a chance at survival.

Everyone made a great fuss over Tad and his ravings. He was bundled into a car to be rushed to a hospital. A few cars went racing off as if to clear the way; others followed as if to pay servile homage to the idiot.

Inside of half an hour I was quite alone with the soft moan of the wind, with the polite curiosity of one goldfinch.

And it was then I went again to the library door.

Again I knocked, calling again as I did so, 'Martha?'

'Come in,' she answered.

40

I left my shotgun propped in the doorway. Martha was accustomed to the semi-dark and could see me: I entered from the daylight and was blind. I knew from her silence that she was watching, waiting; and I knew where she waited.

I felt my way along the bookshelves, touching what I recognized as an ivory ring for decorating harness, knocking a handful of rivets to the floor. I kicked a spittoon. I flung myself blindly on to my knees at the foot of the long leather couch. And in the darkness that was mine if not hers I spoke as gently as ever I might: 'Don't be frightened of me.' I knew that she was exhausted, a little bit uneasy. She must be quite out of her mind with concern at all the shooting she had heard. I touched her feet with my parched lips.

She did not stir. She did not send me away or call me nearer. I trembled to know her will.

In the intensity of my concentration I could hear the heart that knocked in my chest. Now I touched only the leather on which she lay: and yet my fingers knew the fragile odour of her skin. It was warm in the room; she lay uncovered. And in the darkness she reached and put her hand on mine.

It was then I found the courage to act. I slid my fingers along her thigh. Her legs were so immensely long I felt I must forever slide and inch my fingertips towards their fulness. 'Martha, Martha,' I whispered, as if the Muse herself tore words from my throat. 'I won't let them hurt you.'

And then I found that, like me, she wore no underclothes in bed. How could I help but touch those softly curling hairs I had so long remembered from our evening on the beach? My fingers rested warm, for her thighs, with the slightest motion, were no longer together. Her hand was touching my ears, my neck.

I had somehow got halfway on to the couch. She pressed me to the comfort of her nipples and I took one, then the other, then the first again, into my kissing and greedy mouth. 'Don't cry,' was all she said to my hunger. And after what seemed an endless time I heard her saying, 'Don't cry, Demeter. It will be all right.'

I brushed my tears from her breasts with the touch of my tongue. 'Don't worry,' I whispered. 'I can control myself.'

'What day is this?' she whispered in reply. 'Demeter. What is the day?'

'It is only the beginning,' I told her. 'We will have time.'

'My God,' she said. 'Demeter. You must take me—take me—away.'

I had, even while we spoke, fumbled open my fly: and now it was not my hands but hers that found myself: and I didn't then know if she would guide me, stop me, holding my body in the gracious cup of her white hand.

And I will never know.

162

For the first cry came from the rooms beyond the library: the exquisitely piercing mortal cry, the cry half horse, half man, the horse-man cry of pain or delight or eternal celebration at what is and what must be.

I could not restrain myself. I leaped from the couch and dashed into the dining room.

The five mares cowered together as if in terror, fighting to get through a closed window.

I ran into the parlour.

Poseidon ran in a tight circle in the huge parlour, his shod hoofs knocking on the hardwood floor.

'Easy, boy,' I said. 'Easy, Poseidon.'

The huge blue stallion, his breath coming in quick nervous snorts, his short tail held high, ran in dizzying circles. The legs pumped high and strong.

And in the middle of the room on the floor lay the figure of a man.

Yellow-white froth that had dripped from the mouth of the horse now covered the right shoulder of Hazard Lepage. He lay motionless; but even as I shouted and started towards him he raised his head.

Poseidon lunged straight at me. He struck me a glancing blow and I staggered back to the protection of the doorway and the little hall. I went back again to the door and shouted: 'Hazard! Hazard! Over here. Come to me, Hazard.'

In the middle of the floor, he tried to move. He tried to crawl with his arms, dragging his legs. I saw now the open window through which he had made his stealthy approach.

But I would not accuse him; I dashed once more towards his raised hand.

The stallion charged. He came savagely, with a high piercing ear-smashing whinny. Brutally he hit the door as I dodged away; his teeth caught at the wood. He turned and his two hind hoofs smashed a hole in the patterned wall. He went up on his hind legs over the motionless figure of Hazard, and landed astride the man.

Martha Proudfoot was at my side. She handed me the twelve-gauge shotgun, loaded and cocked. 'Kill him!' she cried. 'Please, please, for God's sake, kill him!'

41

'No!' I said.
  But I took the gun.
  'No,' I said. 'No.'
  I stood in the doorway with the cocked gun raised in my hands.
  'Kill him,' Martha pleaded.
  The stallion, trembling, waited now beside the silent form. His great head went down; he sniffed, his breath stirring the torn shirt on Hazard's back. A flicker of muscle ran along the wide, veined belly like a flash of lightning. The whitish-blue hairs were soaked with sweat. The great penis, black fading to pink, dangled half extended from the body.
  'Shoot him,' Martha begged. She was clinging to me; now she was sobbing as she pleaded. Crying.
  The lips of the stallion, long, muscled, touched at the hair on Hazard's head.
  'Come!' I shouted. And then softly: 'Come.'
  The stallion, with a slight touch of a shod hoof, rolled Hazard's figure about like a rag doll. I saw for the first time the bloodied face, and the gun of itself came up; terror raised my gun.
  And over the sight I saw the last and only surviving stallion of the Lepage breed of horse.
  I looked away and Hazard's eyes were open and looking nowhere and yet watching the horse's head.
  'Kill him,' Martha whispered. 'Kill him.'
  'No,' I answered.
  'Kill him now. Hazard is still breathing.'
  'He's all that Hazard lived for,' I said.
  'No,' Martha said.

164

And I thought of firing the gun: in my mind's eye the neck twisted and the head went sideways and up. The stallion fell and rolled over, kicking at the air. A grotesque dance of love: as if the world had turned, not the stallion. The great penis shrank back into the body of the dying horse. The calks of the horseshoes, bright, flashed with the kicking at the lions and the fleurs-de-lis.

'No,' I said. 'Martha—'

And Hazard stirred then, trying once more to move across the floor. I swear he shook his head at the raised gun.

And then it was too late for me to fire: the two heads were together, the man's, the stallion's. The stallion's yellow teeth closed on the arm of the man.

And Hazard Lepage flew upward through the air as if he were a spirit rising to the sky; but his body came back to earth, under the sickening crunch of the stallion's hoofs.

I fired the gun. I pulled both triggers at once. I blew a hole in the stained ceiling. The stallion turned, rearing, and was gone in a great leap and crash through the bay window.

Martha and I raced to Hazard's side. I turned him over before I threw up.

Only Martha looked at the crushed and flayed and formless face. The formless head.

42

I must here intrude a little scientific jargon into an otherwise straightforward account of the life and death of Hazard Lepage. PMU is an abbrevation that enables one to avoid saying Pregnant Mares' Urine. From the urine of pregnant mares (to be more precise, from urine collected during the fifth to the ninth month of the eleventh-month pregnancy), scientists are able to extract the female hormone known as oestrogen. With oestrogen, in turn, they have learned to prevent the further multiplication of man upon the face of the earth.

I do not wish for a moment that my own martyrdom should enshrine me in the hearts of a grateful population. I have pursued the truth in my own way, and let fate fling what darts it will, truth is its own reward. The fickle finger be damned. I need no bronze statues as a sop to the recurring mud. And no one expects to be loved.

Surely those PMU farms that dot the plains of Alberta are memorial enough to my foresight and courage. Each barn contains an average of fifty mares, standing in two neat rows that face each other, harnessed with an ingenious device not unlike a cornucopia so that their urine might run through long clear sterilized tubes under their bellies, then be collected in neat square one-gallon plastic containers.

One mare yields from two-thirds to three-quarters of a gallon of urine per day. The farmer sells that product at approximately $1.95 per gallon, depending of course on the nature of his contract and immediate market conditions. A mare might in one season produce enough to gross the farmer $350.00. He will have to buy $10.00 worth of straw and $40.00 worth of oats. He will have to lay out a little money for mineral supplement (seaweed kelp), for the mare is allowed no salt and little protein. And each mare, let me repeat, *must be pregnant.*

It was the Lepage stallions (and they are renowned as pissers) that filled the vacuum left by the near extinction of the horse. With the scientific breakthrough came a great demand for the service of the male. Each old Percheron mare, every mangy Clydesdale, every Belgian, Appaloosa, Hackney, Thoroughbred, Suffolk Punch, Shetland pony and what have you must be bred and bred often: for the nominal $13.00 stud fee.

Thus you see that for a modest profit to the enterprising farmer, mankind has been delivered from itself. I cannot in all modesty take the entire credit; Hazard Lepage's own persistence through six generations was a contributing factor. But thanks to me, dear Poseidon was shortly after his master's demise to become the busiest creature in all of Alberta.

I was first to recognize that Hazard's accident must be reported at once to the police, and accordingly I started out to walk to the nearest farmhouse and a telephone. What Martha thought or did while I was gone, I cannot imagine. I only know she refused to leave the body.

I might have been gone for two hours had not a Cadillac come bouncing down the trail towards me. I had walked hardly a mile. I was half out of breath from my haste; I expected to be set upon by another band of ruffians from the town of Coulee Hill.

Instead, a very kindly gentleman in a broad-brimmed hat and a beard and a suit and tie stopped beside me and asked courteously if I knew where he might find a Mr Hazard Lepage.

'Mr Lepage,' I told him, 'is deader than a bushel basket of mackerel.'

'Ah yes—' And at that moment I noticed the huge hand on the steering wheel was missing two fingers. 'Then you are referring to the Mr Lepage who raised stallions?'

'The same,' I replied. 'The stallion survives him.'

'Thank heavens,' Mr Utter continued. 'I've been dickering with a Montana firm to provide a certain balm and ointment by the gallon. Unfortunately, this precious fluid must come from pregnant mares . . .'

Need I elaborate?

He was absolutely bursting with excitement at the prospects that were opening before him. Scurrilous, barbarous, stinking man would soon be able, in the sterility of his own lust, to screw himself into oblivion, to erase himself like a rotting pestilence from the face of God's creation: Utter and I surely saw eye to eye on that issue.

We found Martha weeping in the library. The body of Hazard lay where it had fallen, covered by a horse blanket; I used a four-tined fork to clean up the floor just a little, pitching the carefully gathered manure through the broken bay window. When finally the police arrived, they packed off both the corpse and me.

That Eugene Utter and Martha went on to flourish in a most extravagant manner I must assert from hearsay. Only once in all the years of my fidelity have I been acknowledged by Martha and her consort (surely Utter is not to be thought her true husband) to exist, and that when a further opportunity arose for my humiliation. Martha bore one child, a beautiful daughter (conceived in the icehouse, by my calculations; Martha, unlike her mares, chanced to be in full heat). That same daughter, I was informed by telegram, was christened Demeter.

D. Lepage, she now calls herself; and she has grown up to be something of a lover of the horse. To that same girl, as a kind of fatherly advice, I dedicate this portentous volume.